UNDER
RADAR

UNDER

RADAR

Michael Tolkin

Grove Press / *New York*

The lines on p. vii are from *The Collected Poems of Amy Clampitt* by Amy Clampitt, copyright © 1997 by the Estate of Amy Clampitt. Used by permission of Alfred A. Knopf, a division of Random House, Inc.

Published simultaneously in Canada
Printed in the United States of America

FIRST GROVE PRESS EDITION

Library of Congress Cataloging-in-Publication Data
Tolkin, Michael.
Under radar / by Michael Tolkin.—1st ed.
p. cm.
ISBN 0-8021-3990-6 (pbk.)
1. Americans—Jamaica—Fiction.   2. Insurance crimes—Fiction.
3. Married men—Fiction.   4. Murderers—Fiction.   5. Prisoners—
Fiction.   6. Revenge—Fiction.   I. Title.
PS3570.O4278 U53 2002
813'.54—dc21   2002016390

Design by Laura Hammond Hough

Grove Press
841 Broadway
New York, NY 10003

03   04   05   06   07   10   9   8   7   6   5   4   3   2   1

For Maurice Sendak
after a long conversation one August
and
Steve Miller
who helped continue the thought a few days later

                              . . . I fled
offended into worsening weather,

wrapped in a flapping gale's
extravagance, the vestment of an id
that's not at home, that finds no comfort
other than in visions of disaster,

fire, famine, slaughter, shipwreck:
it's there in all of us . . .
                —from "Dejection: A Footnote"

past the earthlit
unearthly masquerade

(we shall be changed)

a silence opens

                —from "A Silence"

                —Amy Clampitt

One

When he was twenty, Tom went to a party where a witch told him, "You will be found out." Some years later, before he was caught, Tom was on a plane to Jamaica.

He had two little girls. Perri was nine and Alma was four. Tom wanted to take the family skiing, but his wife, Rosalie, thought that the routines of ski school, in and out of the cold, the agony of lost mittens, the struggle with ability, would give Alma tantrums, so Tom agreed with— or rather, conceded to—his wife, that the children would be happier in a warm ocean, on an island like Jamaica; and, never having been there, they went. They planned to stay for two weeks.

Rosalie accepted a travel agent's recommendation for the Montego House because all of the hotel's rooms were apartments, with a bedroom, small kitchen, and living room. The hotel assigned every family a baby-sitter, a local woman given the quaintly offensive title "Girl Friday." When Betty, who met them at registration and showed them to their apartment, proved cold and unhappy, Tom agreed with Rosalie that rather than talk to the woman about her bad mood, or ask the resort's manager to replace her with someone who smiled, even artificially, they would keep her, so the children, in their first extended contact with a black woman, would have to fight for affection instead of collecting it as part of the Montego House all-inclusive package, along with free use of snorkels.

On the second day, Rosalie sent a postcard to the travel agent, thanking him.

Dear Otto,
It's glorious here. The children are happy. You were right, the ginger beer is addictive.

Tom had his own sour opinion, too brutal for a postcard. Though he knew from all of his travels not to trust his ill humor on arrival until he had slept a full night, his first tour around the hotel, past the swimming pool, the beach, and the central bar gave him little hope that his mood would improve. He hated the Montego House for all the reasons Rosalie adored it, for what appealed most to a good mother: it was safe for children. Were Tom to send a postcard, he would have listed his complaints against the hotel's bourgeois want of eccentricity, would have said that it was homey, with no sex, with none of the drama of sex. He'd seen the brochures for other resorts, with packs of horny modern women out for the orgy, and the men who hunt them, ballplayers, contractors, young doctors, guys with cash, guys who exercise so they can look like ballplayers. If this had been a family hotel for the very rich . . . but it wasn't. Everyone at the Montego House was comfortable without being wealthy, and this annoyed Tom, because he had a lot of money and he could have afforded a first-class resort with a bigger pool and room service. It was Rosalie who chose this, to save her children from a luxury that would forever spoil them for modest pleasure.

When Tom said to Rosalie after that first cruise around the grounds, "You know what this is? I figured it out. There's a brilliant conspiracy out there that had us committed to a minimum-security prison for families," Rosalie told him to shut up.

It was easy for Tom to comply, since there was so much that he kept secret from his wife.

He didn't play tennis, he didn't play golf, but he did have a sport. On every vacation he always found a woman to secretly cast in a complicated story he built for his own entertainment, he always fixed his attention on a stranger in order for the trip to develop within its morbidly predictable and cloistered order the possibility of possibility, no matter how imaginary, from which he could draw some distracting energy. He had never had an affair after marrying Rosalie, and had very little experience with women before her. No, the whole structure of the game was hidden from the world. He never crossed the boundary to the point where fantasy made a dent on matter, and he always burned, by vacation's end, his dense unwritten novel of travel, secret meetings, murder, punishment, and passionate enlightenment.

He understood that he might be a very sick man. He persisted anyway.

Looking for a secret movie star, Tom strolled by the pool, dividing the mothers into categories. There were the good mothers, always attentive about settling their children's quarrels, married to the good men, fathers who changed diapers, threw the ball, and, without being asked, went back to the room for sunscreen; a few good mothers married to the wrong men, fathers who played deaf to their children's appeals for play; a few sets of bad parents whose children screamed and cried and got their way; and one divorced mother with her quiet son. What an awful place for a divorced mother! There wasn't a single man anywhere, not even a single father. Of course not; the single dads were at the sexy hotels. All of the men at the Montego House were with their wives. They were here because they could afford nothing better, and they could afford nothing better because they were good parents, because they put family ahead of work, taking the world as it came to them, and this timidity or acceptance, the frame in which they embraced their lives, outlined the limit of their ambition. Tom found them, like all the genially cooperative people of the world, impossible to talk to. "I can't talk to these people, they're so emotionally sterile," he said to Rosalie, which she took as the start of a fight:

"I told you not to do this to yourself. Have a drink and relax."

He couldn't follow her advice because he wasn't drinking, which made things worse, made him unappealing. Standing at the bar sipping cranberry juice and tonic, when he casually mentioned to a few of the dads that he was unhappy with the Montego House, he was disappointed because no one agreed with him or even wanted to hear his theories about the trapped almost-rich. He felt their suspicion. They assumed he was a self-declared recovering alcoholic, and since the hotel's open bar served good brands and the bartenders poured generously, the guests, within their own dull moderation, drank more heavily than they did at home. What they didn't want was anyone's disapproving eye on their third daiquiri of the morning. So it was Tom, sober, who ranted like a drunk. And he had stopped drinking for only a month before the trip, to see if his life felt any different, to see if he could stop the unending noise of his mind. Even though he rarely finished more than two glasses of wine at dinner once or twice a week, he felt polluted by the world, and toxic to himself, and so he wanted to purge his system. After a week the experiment yielded a result: Tom saw no real difference between having a drink and not. Worse, with every desire for a drink that challenged his abstention, he attacked himself using a fervor equal to his self-flagellation for the mildest hangover. If there was no difference, why not enjoy a beer and take a vacation from himself? Even Rosalie told him to drink: "You don't like it here because you're sober for no reason. You're not an alcoholic. You can drink. Have a drink, Tom."

He said he would think about it. He knew that the useless asceticism of his self-denial was feeble, a bargain virtue. By holding to his sobriety for the benefit of his detachment, Tom watched the dissipation of his integrity. So why not have the drink now?

Still he resisted escape; he preferred the constant nudging awareness of his need for a drink, just one or two beers. When he forced sobriety, everything he saw caught an echo or reflection, depending on his perspective, of the broken promise that holds time to substance. These stupid contradictions were lost on the other guests, who smelled his contempt for them and stayed away, sitting in the shade of the thatched roof over the bar, laughing with the bartenders.

So he would pretend to be drunk, to himself. He remembered the merciful benefits of a rum at lunch and located within the streams of his scorn toward everyone there a sappy appreciation for these dull wives, and forged from this a maudlin horniness for them, and convinced himself like a lush at closing time that their unimaginative faces, inclined to magazines and weak novels, hid the greatest perversions. He would save them from their sex-panicked husbands. In his counterfeit booziness, staggering between sympathy and sadness for the mother hens of the Montego House, he scanned the air for signals of lust or desire, hidden in this palace of familial sincerity that cried out to the observant, "I do not love the man I married." What to look for? What mattered? Which of you wants sex in a closet with a stranger? Yonder woman whose expensive haircut matches her ironic Jackie-O-with-Ari sunglasses, makeup during the day, and an especially pretty bag filled with fashion magazines and French suntan lotion? Maybe. How slowly did some women lower themselves to a chaise, how carefully did they arrange their bottles of water, magazines, and tubes of sunscreen? Did they smile inwardly at an idea of their own, not to be shared, a perception, a memory, a retreat from the impossibly uncosmic irritating banality of a swimming pool crowded with spoiled children? The woman reading *Architectural Digest,* why was she a likelier pervert than the woman reading *Cosmopolitan*? And the wider the brim, the more expensive the sunglasses, why, Tom wondered, was he so sure that these details advertised overdue wickedness? Or was theirs a bogus decadence, their broad displays of catalog libido and commercial sensuality a sign of the weakness of their impulse to sin? Were these indications of style only a more refined indication of panic and loneliness, which amplified these mothers' regretful desires into a drama they never really wanted, a drama for which they had no genuine aptitude? Or did they have aptitude but no worthy partners? He pitied the women for their men. What is it about this level of society that produces such dull men, the men of the middle? And why am I different? he asked himself. I can smell depravity on the unhappy wives because I can read the lock on a secret, because I have a secret. Yes, how many of the men here, like me, are ten years past unpunished felonies?

When he was two years out of law school, Tom had joined an old friend, Paul Farrar, in a swindle. Farrar knew three doctors willing to go along on a risky venture, faking accident claims to take money from insurance companies. To complete his plan, Farrar needed a few lawyers. Just as he recruited Tom, and Tom recruited another lawyer, so Farrar's other recruits added the few necessary allies. Tom never knew the names of everyone involved, but Farrar had done his homework carefully and managed the crime with a cautious limit on greed; after the gang made enough money, the partnership broke up. Farrar, a genius of persuasion, insisted that each man at the start admit the evil nature of the endeavor, with no justification, no cynicism; no one could say that the insurance companies deserved this. "We're stealing," said Farrar, "that's all we're doing. We're going to make some money, and then we're going to stop. And to settle the accounts a little, we're going to give some of that money back to the world, as charity." He insisted upon this.

The swindle lasted ten months. The alliances within the group had never been more socially complicated than the conspiracy needed, so they hardly ever met when it was over, having little to talk about except their history. Among the people who knew one another already, Farrar discouraged social connections, on guard against friendships among the wives, which could promote more time shared by the men and might lead to private chats beside the barbecue, one testing the other to see if he was game for another round of big money, which might lead to further crime, which might lead to arrest and then betrayal and the exposure of this careful fraud, and Paul Farrar's arrest. Tom was certain that Farrar would have killed to save himself. Seven years on, the statue of limitations had passed and they were free in the eyes of the law. Farrar joked, "With time off for good behavior, we'd be getting out about now."

Tom liked to talk to Farrar about the implications of living with the memory of sin; it was one of Tom's favorite subjects, how the knowledge of an unpunished crime grinds a lens through which the world looks small and more easily managed. Paul noted to Tom that of the four marriages in the group, there had been no divorces. "I picked right," said Farrar. "Everyone I picked was stable."

They knew that guilt destroys some men, and Tom credited Farrar for refusing to pretend that their occasional streams of bad feeling weren't guilt. Each of them discovered that the world made more sense, knowing that anyone they met might just as easily have a secret such as theirs. Over the years, as the crime passed into a dimming legend even in his own dossier, Tom confessed small pieces of it to new friends, or alluded to his villainous past in a way that gave the impression he was talking about a few years wasted on drugs, hardly a special event, but he cast his net with a careful intonation when he wanted to test a hunch with someone he suspected of his own criminal story. He didn't expect anyone to suddenly tear the wrapping off his secret any more than Tom would have opened up. If the other was as vigilant against exposure as Tom, he would, with tact and speed, move the discussion to neutral territory. Then Tom knew. Skilled deflection was the giveaway.

What if he pushed himself to one of the women by the pool and said straight to her face, "Listen to this carefully: a lot of people don't get caught, and sometimes there's no way to look at a man and guess his crime, but let him lift the veil on his own past, just a little, and when you know your own felony, you can see it on him like a tattoo." What then?

Five days into the vacation, and none of the women had yet dragged a fantasy out of him. And then on the sixth day, the airport bus delivered her.

With hair short as Joan of Arc's, the woman on whom Tom would fix his fantasy sat with her feet in the water, reading an ancient edition of *Sense and Sensibility*. The book had a faded hunter-green cover, with the title embossed in a chipped gold. She wore a wedding ring and a small diamond. Tom was jealous of the woman's husband. Here was a woman careless enough to risk staining a rare book with suntan oil, just for the pleasure of reading a nineteenth-century novel in a nineteenth-century binding. What a wife she must be! What a companion! How well must she encourage her husband if she allows herself such a violation of custom. There's a husband who can share his secrets with his wife! But why are they here? The husband of such a woman, wouldn't he be a greater success than the rest of the men at the Montego House, elevated by his wife's beauty, confidence, taste, and careless attachment to precious things, wouldn't he have the wealth for a suite at the Four Seasons, or a villa with a staff and room for his friends? Or was Tom's little movie of their success the payoff for an ambition she could have helped her man achieve, but together, servants of the highest moral style, they had rejected? Did she teach him that she was all the prize a man could want? Did she reward him for leaving the office in time for dinner with the children, helping them with their homework, reading poetry in bed? She could love him so well that her love tamed his striving after the real cost of the Four Seasons' fluffy towels and twenty-four-hour in-room dining. There's a noble wife for these greedy days, there's the woman of valor! Take the rare book to the beach because you want to. Don't work so hard that you miss the pleasures of the moment.

Tom watched her turn the page, slowly. From what service of devotion other than a love of precious things— like this book—and the freedom to lose them, damage them, could he recognize a woman whose conversation would surely slide from erudition to the capricious to the risqué to bed? She was everything he had ever needed from a stranger. The intrigue of her signs melted his brain; her combination of fashion and literature, narcissism and intellect, made her the closest thing at the beach to Paris. Had she cut her hair for comfort? He hoped not. He wanted her to have almost shaved her head for a purpose so complicated that her motivation was deeper than she might know; he wanted her to have cut that gorgeous hair in defiance of the world, to deny the raving famished beast of the world the morning milk of her beauty. He might have broken a window with his hand if he thought that by cutting her hair this woman's sacrifice was also cruel, to protect her man from the sin of adoring something she could lose, to ruin the revered crown of her beauty and diminish her beloved husband's strength for work, destroying his shot at marriage-wrecking wealth.

Tom tried to read her more deeply and studied her for ten happy minutes like a birdwatcher in a rookery. Now the full scene at the pool, so loud and annoying without this woman, giggled with the life of children in water. Nothing had changed except Tom's fervor.

Without warning, the woman's children hugged her from behind: her daughter, Tom guessed six; and a boy, probably four, whose Girl Friday brought them to her for just those kisses, on their way to the children's buffet. When they toddled off, the woman with short hair set the book down and leaned back to do stomach crunches, lifting her feet out of the water and pumping her legs in and away. Was she showing off? Good. Was she bored? Even better. What theater did she hope the attention would open? He tried to add up what excited him about her, and weave into this the elements of the day, the heat, the heavy wet air, and the fumes of his second imaginary rum punch. Taking these things together, he convinced himself that she was a rare free spirit with a profound inner life like his, and if so, she would be available to him if he found the right words.

When he passed by, she stirred a little, and he knew that she knew, without knowing exactly why, that someone wanted her. He was certain that the Jane Austen of Jamaica felt all of this secret attention as a subtle pressure in the air from Tom's direction, and from then on that day, even as his furthest stray thought retrieved a mental image of her when she was somewhere else in the resort, she would look over her shoulder.

In bed that night, Rosalie said, "You're finally relaxing."

"Yes," he said. "It always takes me a while. I'm sorry."

"That's why vacations last a few weeks. You work hard, you need a lot of time to find yourself."

The next afternoon Tom saw Jane Austen's husband walking on the beach with the little boy and girl. Tom thought at first that this fat man in a pink Lacoste shirt, lime-green Bermuda shorts, brown socks, and black sandals, this sweating parody of the revolting American tourist, was only a friend, but the little boy called him Daddy and held his hand, chattering about octopus tentacles, and what happens if you cut off the tentacle of an octopus, and does the tentacle grow back? So Jane Austen, the best inspiration this stupid resort could offer him, was married to an oaf. If he was going to give himself a fever over a stranger, he wanted a worthy rival to illustrate the dust jacket, a handsomely corrupt pirate standing defeated in the background while Tom made love to his lady. He wanted someone who threatened him, a lean man with the perceptive gaze of a flight instructor, a judge of character, a man who could size you up and, by the way you stood at ease or agony when no one was watching, judge even your father. But then a thought gave Tom fuel for his fantasy: the fat man and Jane Austen were lying, this marriage was all for show. She was his slave and would never see her real husband again, that man of muscle and sinew, if she didn't cooperate. Tom found himself rescuing Jane Austen from the demonically obese kidnapper only to return her to her grateful thin husband, a pediatric eye surgeon working among the poor in Haiti.

If this were so, thought Tom, how could I signal to her that I was here to help? I could tell her about Ira. I could sit beside her at the pool, and I could say, "I used to have a friend named Ira. He inherited a construction business from his father. He was always late to meetings, and he was lazy and slow and the business failed. He was fat. I'll tell you the truth, I used to bore my wife with all the excuses I made for Ira, because Ira was my friend. Even though he came to his mother's funeral in a hooded blue sweatshirt, I wanted to help him. One day he asked me to loan him money so he could buy an industrial coffee roaster, so he could open a coffee business. My wife said that if I wanted to throw my money away, I should at least buy the industrial coffee roaster myself and then lease it to him, so if he went bust I'd have something to sell. Of course the business died, what do you expect, because Ira was a loser. I sold the machine at a loss, but this was good for me, a tuition payment on experience. In the difference between the price and the damage, I stopped justifying Ira's failures. I stopped having sympathy for Ira. I stopped looking at his inanimate bulk as the expression of some pain that made him such a disaster at business, at love, at friendship. Would you like to know why? Because of my wife. My wife didn't see obesity as a problem. She pointed out to me the many fat men in the world who transcend all of Ira's most unfortunate attributes: a thick nose, small eyes, big stomach, dying hairline; men with stunning women, maybe their wives, maybe just women they fuck. I saw these men, these larded medieval Jew barons, I had always seen them, but denied the implication of what they proved, to protect my buddy Ira.

"No longer. I'm a connoisseur now, and we have a name for these men: my wife and I call these men the Realized Iras. Realized Iras are otherwise grotesque men of commerce whose vivacious appetites make them sexually attractive, whose expansive capacities for money, food, pleasure, and friendship intimidate the world. And if I were going to leave my wife for you, Jane Austen, even in fantasy, your fat man would be a Realized Ira, not the sunburned sloth who made you his slave. Your alleged husband has no tone, no buoyancy, none of the elastic grace of the Realized Iras, and he has none of that grace in his heart," which is why Tom killed him for what he did the awful night of the Reggae Party, after Tom had already resigned his tangled daydream.

Two

I t happened on the eighth night of the trip, when Tom was trying to make the best of things. He took his daughters swimming in the ocean every day, giving Rosalie the time to rest. This commitment yielded his marriage an allowance for gladness. He began to relax. He encouraged himself to see his surrender of Jane Austen as his triumph over an addiction to distraction. Rosalie, sensing a change in Tom's relationship to life, from sullen detachment to quiet acceptance, soon hugged him in pure appreciative companionship. "I love you, Tom," she told him. "Tom, I really love you. You're so good, and I've been so bad. I have to apologize, I've been distant, I've been cold, and I see you with the girls, and I realize how much I've been withholding from the three of you. I'll try to be better." So she blamed herself, the chill between them was her fault, blind to the price he made Rosalie pay for his passion for Jane Austen. He might have told her that the fault was his but considered that perhaps Rosalie was confessing in her own oblique way to sins he never suspected. He could have said, "Look,

Rosalie, it's not just you, it's me. I have my crimes, what
are yours?" No, give her privacy. He hoped she was telling the truth in her own way, to relieve herself of a burden. He thought he could read her mind, which told him,
"We always try to hide the secret of our lives. What I believe to be the hidden core of my life will not easily be
deciphered, even when I give a hint, as in this shy apology, to the outer circumstances." He loved her for this,
and he hugged her close, and when she said, again, "Tom,
I'm sorry," he found a heavy tear that fell down his cheek,
for he was crying in gratitude, crying in praise.

They went to dinner. The girls ate with all the other
children on a different terrace, watched over by the nan-
nies. Rosalie brought Tom to a table with a woman she
was excited about, Avital Davis, an American who lived
in Jerusalem with her husband, an Israeli, who was at
home. Avital was here with her parents and sister and her
sister's family, all from Cincinnati, for their annual reunion. Everyone was agreeable: the two sisters, women
of attractive high intelligence and culture, and their parents, serious and attentive, taking their place in an un-
forced easy way with a younger generation. The mother
was a labor lawyer. The father was a judge, and Tom, for
the first time that week, found himself in conversation
with a man he admired. Tom, in turn, felt Judge Davis's
interest, curiosity, and respect. The men let the women
talk about children and education while they talked about
jail. They came to the subject easily. Judge Davis had
many things to say about the breakdown of the prison

system, which fascinated Tom, who did not tell the judge that his obsession with life behind bars was not just academic. He craved to know what his life would have been like if the conspiracy failed and the men were arrested. Here was the syndicate's weakness; Farrar swore the men never to tell their wives. "Call me when you want to talk about it—at any time of the day or night—if you can't bear your guilt, but don't tell your wives." Farrar was a genius, and a genius is someone who understands men, one at a time. Though they trusted Farrar and wanted his admiration, Tom composed a fugue of betrayal in which one of the doctor's wives, suspicious of her husband, discovers his hidden money, and then the crime, and, in a fit of ethics, leaves him, hires a divorce lawyer, himself an ethical man who encourages her to bring her evidence to the district attorney's office, and she, made horny by her lawyer's integrity (in Tom's imagination, he's in a wheelchair), falls in love with him while informing on her husband, devoting the rest of her life to the service of this honest invalid. She leads a fight for the rights of the handicapped while Tom is in jail.

Nothing like this happened, but stories about prison were Tom's pornography.

"Did you send many men to jail?" Tom asked.

"Well, yes, I did," said the judge.

Tom waited for him to say more. Judge Davis waited for a better question. Tom found one, not a question but a way into the subject. "It's a fascinating subject."

"Carry some guilt, do you?" Tom saw the judge treat the word lightly, this was Jew-to-Jew talk about the emotional scars of a particular childhood, not a hint of insight into Farrar's conspiracy.

"You're very shrewd. I suppose I do."

"It's typical." Typical of what? The more reassuring word would have been "normal."

"Does prison help?" asked Tom.

"You mean, does the shock of the system cure some criminals of their crimes?"

"Something like that."

"I think I know what you're asking," said the judge. "You've read some articles about the expanding prison population."

"Yes."

"And you're aware that while more money is being spent on prisons, the cash goes to contractors and guards, not to any rehabilitation programs."

"Right," said Tom, with a mixture of relief and embarrassment for his awkward phrasing of something Judge Davis could put so simply, and his shame for the way his morbid fascination with prison could come out only in such a squeak, while behind the misshapen presentation of himself something inexpressible cramped the flow of thoughts.

"But this assumes," continued the judge, warming to an audience, "that the main function of prison has to be a cure for crime, something other than punishment, or punishment that also protects."

"Protects who?"

"You and me," said the judge. He looked hard at Tom, because Tom had just confused the criminal with the victim. Tom was thinking about prison as a place where the criminals are protected from their victims. Now he was sure that Judge Davis, drunk but no fool, saw this blending as the real reason for Tom's questions. Yes, thought Tom, he knows I am guilty of something real.

"I meant that prison can protect the criminal from the people he hurt, the people who would want revenge." Boy, did that sound odd.

"That's a novel thought for a lawyer."

Tom felt the judge drifting with him into incoherence. He stammered, "And then, and then, you know, there's rehabilitation. Not to mention his punishment. I mean, not to mention that he's being punished. That is . . . you know, he's given the chance to, you know, look at where he is, and maybe decide that when he gets out, he doesn't want to go back because . . . jail is so horrible, and it is horrible, jail, isn't it?"

The judge dropped his congeniality. "I'm a liberal Jew, Tom, but I don't believe in rehabilitation for all but a few, in fact, for such a few that when I look at the individual cases of those who returned to the path of lawfulness, I see men whose returns were promised in their falls, and that's a small group of men, Tom, whose crimes were spiritual crises, almost artistic crises. The average thief and rapist, the average killer, however much and perhaps because he was so damaged by society and conditioning, is too wounded and broken, too sick, too stupid, for any restoration of decency. Lock them up, Tom. Did I say stupid? Yes, I did. Do I sound cruel? I've sent three men to their death, Tom. You didn't ask about that. And I can sleep at night."

While the men talked, the children's dinner ended. Tom paid some attention to Alma and Perri as they followed the fleet of children to the broad wooden deck beyond the dining room, where the hotel band played on a low stage. One extension of the deck was built on stilts over a rock shelf, which the water just covered at high tide. Then the children raced from one side of the deck to the other, to the few triumphant dying waves, inches tall, that succeeded from the bay. This gave the parents great happiness, the giddy shrieks of their children blended with the sounds of ocean and kitchen, every property of the evening resonant and clear, each fragrant piece of it, sound, vision, and emotion, suspended in a Jell-O of gently drunken satisfaction.

Alma loved music, and when the bass player or the pianist first tested the volume, she left the wave chasers. Alma, at four, was happy as soon as the musicians arrived in the little shack. She was old enough to know that the tuning and the busying with volume and balance were not yet the show, but was fascinated by all the efforts that she could not yet explain. Alma liked men, but she didn't know that she did; the power of the musicians was not just in their music and the skill from which the music flowed but from the stunning—to a four-year-old—

difference and presence and distinction of their sex. And then they were black, and their blackness was of a piece with the strangeness of their skills, the strangeness of their quiet assembly among the loud instruments. She didn't know that the house musicians were only adequate at what they did, that house bands, in the bargain for a steady job, trade away the possibility of a larger audience that can be theirs only if the audience is not captive. Like all house bands, they tested and then abandoned their original songs a few times, since the hotel's guests weren't there to hear that specific band but rather a set of generally familiar songs. Every night the band played roughly the same set, which always included "I Shot the Sheriff," "Jumping Jack Flash," "Michelle," and a synthesizer-steel-band-calypso version of "Cheek to Cheek." This repetition of old hits usually makes for sloppy music, but the house band had a sense of humor, which made them cynical, so they amused one another. This made them entertaining.

The band played, and Alma stood to the side, watching them. The judge continued to pound away at Tom. "As for punishment, our society chooses boredom over humiliation. I suspect that if we publicly scourged our criminals every now and then, some categories of crime might be less popular."

Alma jumped up and down to the music behind in a line of other little girls.

The judge: "It'd work like gangbusters for your white-collar types, I can assure you of that, much more so than it would on the poor. A man needs bread, or money for his drugs, and in the heat of his necessity, he'll do what he must, careless of which consequence lies in wait. But you and I have chewed that crust already. You take a lawyer who's pulled some kind of con, and you lead him into the town square and lay on fifteen good ones with a cat-o'-nine-tails, and I bet you that up on the forty-ninth floor, after that spectacle, there'll be some serious hesitation about cutting the legal corners. And I would love to extend this to public officials who take bribes. But what do you think? Do you see many dirty lawyers?"

Tom was distracted by the way Alma was dancing now; she was in front of the other girls, closer to the singer, who seemed to be singing directly to her. This might have been charming, but Tom was uncomfortable with the singer's connection with his daughter, he wasn't treating her like a little girl. He was singing to her like she was a woman. Tom wanted to stop this, but he had the judge's question to answer.

"Malpractice isn't my specialty. I do wills and trusts. It's all very dry."

"With your interest in such things," said the judge, while the singer was bumping and grinding and Alma was responding, "you might want to expand your practice. Curiosity and obsession are the best mentors."

"I don't know if it's an obsession."

"I think it is. That's not a crime. Wills and trusts are pretty far from helping drug dealers wash their dirty money."

"I don't do that," said Tom, about to get up. He tried to catch Rosalie's eye. She was deep in a huddle with the judge's wife and daughter, and he didn't want to make a scene.

"Of course you don't. You wouldn't be staying here with such a lovely wife."

Tom took "lovely wife" to be a thought of pure condescension. The judge, having uncovered from Tom's slips of conversation the evidence of his criminality, saw a dull minor felon and reduced the sentence; Rosalie was not the glamorous hetaera who anneals herself to the serious bad guy, so if Tom was guilty of a punishable offense, it must have been small potatoes. Tom also read that the judge, after all of his years on the bench, had come to envy something in the criminal parade, nothing so easy as to say the freedom of the outlaw, but there was a kind of fabulous woman who, by her endorsement of an incriminated man, made Judge Davis repent his own pious authority and moral virtue. The judge could have said "beautiful," but the beauties as he knew them were linked to men whose wealth afforded them the next level of luxury, at the resort hotels with full service spas and big bathtubs and thick robes meant for courtesans.

The singer was fucking the air across the dance floor from Tom's little girl. "Excuse me," said Tom, rising. He knew he was giving Judge Davis the impression that he had left the table to escape his insight.

Surrounded by a shameless audience, Alma stood alone on the dance floor, six feet from the singer, shaking her body to mirror his moves. The singer stabbed his hips toward her, he was fucking her for laughs, and she answered him in her own spastic way. She followed his lead, possessed by the music and the encouraging laughter and applause of the crowd. Jane Austen's fat husband was nearby, and as Tom ran to take Alma from the floor, Perri came up to him and said, "That man," meaning Mr. Austen, "told Alma to dance."

What an ugly thing, to see my daughter made into this joke, thought Tom. What a disgusting thing for everyone to think it's so funny that my daughter is innocent of the implications of her beauty and energy and love of music and movement. What evil people let a four-year-old roll her hips like this for their cheap amusement?

Tom rushed through the children dancing at the edge of the floor and took Alma in his arms. She kicked him. "I want to dance!" she cried.

"Honey, that's enough."

"No!" She kicked him again, then punched him. Now everyone was laughing at Tom. He wanted to scream at them. Pagans! he wanted to say. This is child sacrifice, he wanted to say, burning a child's dignity for laughs.

The singer didn't stop. Tom pulled Alma out of the circle and brought her to the rail at the edge of the deck. The sound of gravel rolled by the sea like wind in tall grass, calming both of them.

"I want to dance," she said, but the fury was gone. Tom thought that she was grateful for the rescue.

"You danced enough."

"Why did you take me away?"

"The band was loud, and I didn't want the music to hurt your ears."

She accepted this. It was often easy for Tom and Rosalie to quiet the children with simple lies that addressed the issues in close consonance. It was a lie, but if his four-year-old had not been tricked into dancing like a whore, he might have taken her away anyway, just as he explained. She asked if she could dance where she was, and he said Yes. Now she danced like herself, a free ballerina or figure skater, *en pointe,* back arched and right leg lifted. She rolled her hips and belly in one sexual shudder, as she had on the floor, but Tom kept a blank face and, allowing no response to her lewd gesture, he began to sever the connection between the encouraged concupiscence and the approval of her audience. After this, the charming ballerina took over from Salomé.

All of this happened quickly, and Rosalie joined them.

"Did you see that?" Tom asked quietly, while Alma danced.

"What was she doing?"

"That fat fuck over there"—Tom almost said "Jane Austen's husband," but why give Rosalie a peek into the deeper vaults of the cave?—"told Alma to dance."

"Oh, Alma," said Rosalie, giving her Terpsichore a big hug and picking her up. "You do like to dance, don't you?"

"I was dancing," she said.

"Yes you were."

Rosalie took Alma in her arms, the girl's legs strad-dling her hips. Tom looked his daughter in the eye and saw confusion. She could not articulate what she was feel-ing, but Tom was certain that in her own way she knew that the performance had violated her. Alma had a sense of honor.

"It's over," said Rosalie. "Come back to the table, Tom, the judge loved talking to you."

"In a minute."

"Where are you going?"

"I just want to say something to the guy who told Alma to dance."

"What?"

"I want to tell him that I wish he hadn't."

"Just don't hit him."

"I won't." She was joking. Tom wasn't.

Rosalie carried Alma back to Judge Davis's table. Tom stepped over the legs of some children who sat be-side their parents on the deck. It was all so ordinary. Jane Austen's husband drank a Red Stripe beer, and his head kept time with the music. Tom stood next to him.

"Excuse me," he said, "but did you tell my daughter to get up and dance?" All of this was only five minutes old.

"Your daughter?" asked the man.

"That little girl over there." Tom pointed to Alma, sitting in Rosalie's lap.

"Oh. Yes. She was on the side of the dance floor jumping around, and there were some kids already there, and she seemed kind of shy about it. I thought she wanted to dance with them, so I told her to get out in front and have a good time, not to be shy."

"And you saw what happened."

"She danced. Is there a problem?"

"That was a stupid thing to do. That was inappropriate and stupid. She's four years old."

"I'm not quite sure what you're so upset about, but if it's your family custom not to dance, then I'm sorry, I really am."

"Do you think someone with a family custom against dancing would come to Jamaica?"

"Anything is possible. People make mistakes."

"So who made the mistake here, you or me?"

"Maybe both of us. Why was she alone?"

"She was with her sister."

"What's your name?"

"Tom. Tom Levy."

"Barry Seckler. Tom, whatever I did to offend you, or to offend your daughter, please let it be forgiven. And if you can't, then please explain to me the nature of my crime."

What could Tom say? The man would deftly turn away every accusation, he had that skill, Tom saw, more than that, charm. Charm enough to have a pretty wife with short hair.

"It's over, that's what matters," said Tom, lying. He backed away like an ambassador to royalty, then turned around. Aware that he was onstage now, he walked to the dining terrace.

Tom's world shattered into attributes of color, sound, meaning, memory, taste, touch, opinion, and disinterest. His disinterest in the very attributes he noticed equaled in its vigor the intensity of Judge Davis's wife's T-shirt, turquoise, with the words SANTA FE above an imitation gold-leaf primitive eagle. The shirt made Tom want to kill Jane Austen's husband. What is this fucking bullshit? thought Tom. This fake bullshit notion of purity reserved for a fake bullshit version of Native American religion. The turquoise T-shirt brought to Tom the recognition that all impressions break on contact, that the blue of the shirt had no greater significance than the darkness of the ocean, or the black headwaiter with his shaved head and his white jacket with pink lapels.

The band played "I Shot the Sheriff," and the melody and the instruments drifted into separate universes, though Tom saw each one and stood between, the mediator of all the realities around him.

No good will come of this murder. The thought washed through Tom as directly and with the same dull inevitability as the umpteenth wave chased by the children as it rolled under the deck. The children peered through the spaces between the boards, trying to gauge where on the meridians made by the boards the wave would disperse in a satisfaction for them and for itself. The drama of the wave kept them at the game, the contest of endurance. The children knew that the waves had feeling and intelligence, and when the last peak settled into the last trough, the children saw collapse and relief; the battle was over. The wave says, I can die now, my purpose is known. Or perhaps not, thought Tom, perhaps the wave at the last margin of the ocean hated all of this, the endless duty to the grinding away of the shore, exhaustion cheered by children.

Tom withdrew from the deck and walked back to the dining room, where the waiters were clearing tables and the parents who had formed groups among themselves thought about the picture they made of themselves lingering, how contentment reigned on this Caribbean shore; good enough food and good enough wine consoled the almost rich and abraded them of their roughest feelings, the bad ideas anyone has about life and their place in it. Tom could hear, over the singer and the band, droplets of conversation carried like spume on the damp heavy air of the tropics, not real laughter at anyone's wit so much as punctuation, a way to end a bad thought or rip the conch of conversation from the hands of whoever was telling whatever kind of story. All these people basically like each other, thought Tom. And why shouldn't they? Tom saw all of them as something he could never be, a kind of happy because they all felt the same way; swallow your pride and have a table of new friends for life. And he joined his wife, with his own new friends, and had an answer ready if the judge should ask him about what had just happened.

"What just happened?" asked the judge.

"You see that man over there," said Tom, pointing to Jane Austen's husband.

"Which one?" asked the judge.

"The man in the blue shirt," said Tom. But there were two men in blue shirts. Not prudent to call him fat, since the judge carried a few extra pounds and so did his wife.

"The fat one sitting by the dance floor? Or the other one standing by the light?" the judge asked.

"The fat one."

"What did he do?"

"He told my four-year-old daughter to dance like a stripper."

"He did not," said the judge, but he meant, He did?

"I told him that what he had done was really inappropriate. But I felt like killing him."

"If you'd told me that, I would have stopped you. I would have had to."

"Of course," said Tom. Rosalie was half listening from her end of the table; he heard the woman from Israel talking about schools in Tel Aviv, the world has one problem, thought Tom, it's so simple.

"But I meant that only by Jewish law," said the judge.

"In what way?" asked Tom.

"If you had told me that you were on your way to kill a man, well, you know the Talmudic rule, don't you?"

"I don't think so," said Tom, but he meant, No.

"You should. You're a lawyer and a Jew. Let me tell you a story," said the judge.

The band stopped playing. Silence impermissible, one of the bartenders punched a button on a cassette deck, for more Jamaican music. No one was going to listen to the judge but Tom.

"This is all a long time ago."

...

In Jerusalem, politics; in Jericho, the weather. Simeon and Reuven, in Jericho, were sitting in the shade of the ruined temple to Baal, and agreed that the day was hot, when their friend Naftali ran across the square, chased by a man with a short sword in his right hand. Naftali did not look at the two men as he passed them on the steps. The swordsman lost sight of Naftali and stopped.

"He's in there," said the swordsman.

"I don't think so," said Reuven.

"Is he your friend?" asked the swordsman.

"What did he do?" asked Simeon.

The swordsman was about to answer when the silhouette of Naftali's head appeared along the straight line of a column's shadow and then he jumped through a breach in the temple's rear wall. The swordsman followed him.

There was a scream, and when Simeon and Reuven climbed through the wall, they saw the swordsman standing over Naftali's body. The sword, dripping blood, was in his hand.

Naftali's brothers arrived with a crowd. The swordsman, Avigdor, had been in love with a girl named Timna, but Naftali was going to marry her and the wedding had just been announced.

A court was called for the next day. Reuven and Simeon faced the three judges. The youngest spoke first. "What did you see?" he asked Reuven.

"I saw Avigdor kill Naftali."

"What did you see?"

"I saw Avigdor chase Naftali into the old shrine, I saw Naftali climb through a hole in the wall, and I saw Avigdor follow him. Then my friend and I followed them and saw Avigdor standing over the body."

The judges asked Simeon to tell the story and he told the same story. The case was then dismissed, since the witnesses had seen nothing. However, the judges warned Avigdor to leave immediately for a city of refuge, where Naftali's family could not, for revenge, follow him.

The next day, sitting again on the steps of the shrine, Simeon said to Reuven, "The courts are too strict about this."

Reuven said, "I don't trust a judge who's younger than I am."

He was about to say more when they saw Avigdor running across the square, chased by Naftali's oldest brother, with a long sword in his hand. Avigdor tripped and fell on the steps. Naftali's brother put the sword to his throat.

"Stop!" said Simeon. "Don't you know that if you kill Avigdor, you are liable for execution?"

"I know that," said Naftali's brother.

"What is your name?" asked Simeon.

"Issachar."

"Issachar, do you know what we have to do if you kill him?"

"Yes," he said. Then Issachar put his sword into Avigdor's heart.

When the court met again, Reuven told the story. "We asked Issachar if he knew the law and knew the penalty. He said that he did, and then he killed Avigdor."

On the day of the execution, Simeon and Reuven followed Issachar, wearing a white tunic, his hands tied behind his back.

At the place of execution, the roof of the tallest building in the city, the judges looked to the watchtower on the hill to the west of town, hoping for a signal from the high court in Jerusalem. The signal arrived to proceed with the execution.

The guards led Issachar to the roof's edge, and pulled his tunic away. The youngest judge put a hand on Reuven's and Simeon's shoulders. "I know you don't want to do this," he said.

"Don't apologize for the law," said Reuven.

Simeon waited a moment, and Reuven whispered to him, "Now."

Simeon said, "Issachar, I'm sorry," and pushed hard, before Reuven. Issachar was already falling when Reuven made contact with his sweaty back. Perhaps this is why Issachar turned in the air and landed on his side.

The oldest judge, on the ground, called the men down. Issachar was still alive.

"I don't want to do this," said Simeon.

"Draw lots," said the judge.

"No," said Reuven, "let me finish this."

Issachar's eyes were open, and Reuven saw in them a melting of the humiliation for being naked and broken. The reluctant executioner lifted the chosen rock and smashed it hard on the murderer's chest. Blood seeped from Isaachar's mouth, but he was dead, and the rusty taste of his punishment made no impression.

...

Tom saw Jane Austen talking to the man in charge of island tours at a kiosk near the bar. She was signing her family up for a trip, and wherever she was going with her family, Tom wanted to be with her.

"That's Jewish law for you," said Judge Davis. "Don't kill anyone."

"I won't," said Tom, lying.

"It's a different way of looking at things," said Judge Davis's wife.

This banality gave Tom allowance to leave. He waved his fingers to Rosalie in a semaphore of marriage:

have-to-do-something-be-right-back-don't-ask-good-for-
us-all-I-love-you.

"Excuse me," he said.

"Pleasure talking," said the judge. "I hope we have
more time together."

"I'm sure we will."

Tom walked slowly towards the tour desk, waiting
for Jane Austen to leave before he presented himself to
the man with the name tag: ISAIAH.

"Can I help you?" asked Isaiah.

"I think so," said Tom. "I'd love to take a trip."

"May I recommend the Dunn's River Falls Tour,
and then duty-free shopping in Ocho Rios? That's our
most popular trip. It's half a day."

"Is that what the woman who was just here is
doing?" Tom said this in a way that advertised nothing
more than bewilderment at the choices, a mild despera-
tion at his inability to select from too bountiful a buffet
of possibilities, and his faith that in someone else's endorsement of one choice he might rescue himself from a
confusion too silly to belabor.

"Mrs. Seckler and her family are taking the Scenic
Inland Trip: Bob Marley's birthplace and grave, then
Dunn's River and Ocho Rios. That's a full day."

"Sounds great. I'd like four tickets, two adults, two
kids, one under five."

"You can go the day after tomorrow."

"I'd like to go tomorrow. Why can't I go on their
bus?"

"These are small vans, and they've booked a private tour. You can arrange it for the next day."

"What if the Secklers share the van? Would that lower their cost?"

"Not really, sir. But they might share it anyway."

Jane Austen Seckler was in the gift shop, twenty feet away. "Perhaps you could ask her," said Tom.

"Perhaps *you* could," said Isaiah. "It would be harder for her to turn you down than me."

"And you'd lose the sale."

"I am a businessman, sir, like yourself."

"I'll ask her." Tom walked into the gift shop, the bells on the door announcing him. There she was, Mrs. Seckler, trying on a hat she wouldn't buy.

"Excuse me," said Tom, "but Isaiah at the tour desk suggested I speak to you."

"Yes?" She looked at him politely, with a measure of caution. Had she seen him talking to her husband?

"I understand you're going on the trip to Bob Marley's grave tomorrow morning. I wanted to take that trip, too, and tomorrow's the best day for my family. If it wouldn't be too much trouble, could you share the van?"

"How many are you?"

"There's four of us. Two little girls, and my wife, of course."

"I think that's a good idea. I have two children. They'll fight less with company. I'm Debra Seckler."

"Tom Levy."

"Do I need to say something to the tour desk?"

"I don't think so. He'll trust me."

Tom thanked her again. Isaiah explained that the trip could not be charged to the room, because the tour guides were independent of the hotel, a detail of no special interest to Tom, who paid for the day of murder with his credit card.

Now Tom returned to the table. He kissed Rosalie on the cheek as he greeted Judge Davis. "We're taking a trip tomorrow, the family, into the interior, up in the mountains. Bob Marley's grave. The pictures looked really pretty."

"All day in a car? You should have asked me." Tom wanted to slap her, but of course she was right, a day in the van would do nothing for the children.

"It's all very close. We're only going up to Bob Marley's grave, or, to be less morbid about it, Bob Marley's birthplace, and then down to Dunn's River for a climb in the falls, which the girls should just love, and then some duty-free shopping."

"Except it's not duty-free," said Avital Davis. "The prices are flexible, and if you don't know the cost in New York, you'll pay more."

"Thanks for the tip," said Tom. He caught Rosalie's doubtful eye. "This should be good. This is the kind of trip we like."

The judge weighed in. "I think it would be fascinating. We should go."

Rosalie brightened. "We can go with the Davises."

"I already booked the van, and we're sharing it with another family."

"Is there room for us?" asked Avital.

"I didn't think so. I'm sorry. I should have come to you."

"Let's go with them the day after tomorrow," said Rosalie.

"The ticket's not refundable," said Tom, thinking he was probably lying. "The other couple have two children, a boy and a girl. They'll have fun together."

"Not in a van," said Rosalie.

"At the falls, then. The Dunn's River Falls are beautiful. They've shot a lot of movies there. I think they shot *The Swiss Family Robinson* there."

The group shared vague memories of the film.

"Nonrefundable," said Rosalie, sealing the day. New people would interfere with Rosalie's purpose for the vacation, to spend undistracted time with the girls. She hated to lose contact with them on vacations even as they needed desperately to run free, no matter that the resort was another tightly pressed bale of the world's artifice.

It was time for bed. The families made their farewells. Judge Davis, Tom thought, had let go his suspicions. Tom put his arm around Rosalie; Alma wanted his free hand, Perri held to her mother. Two miles or more offshore—who could judge distance?—a cruise ship with all lights blazing moved to the west, away from the port at Ocho Rios.

He showed the boat to the girls and felt terribly proud of himself, that this family, this little unit of the world, was his, like a ship over the water. It was so obvious to him why people love watching boats, they see themselves as ships under way, and this is a good and wonderful identification. Look at what you can learn from a ship, how to stay bright under a darkening sky, in an uncertain ocean.

Shed of the sullen Girl Friday, the family walked slowly to the room, the girls reaching for him, holding on and letting go, Perri's hand damp and Alma's soft and cool. Tom's decision to kill a man gave him wisdom, because it was a secret. He was good at keeping secrets. How hateful to cross the public square with all your inner life on parade. If one was too bland for an inner life, why not break a rule and create a private universe? Hiding something so powerful gave him dignity.

He would never be a better father than on this walk, witness to his own awesome criminal and loving nature, to the awesome careless and loving nature of his daughters. Slow down, he commanded himself. Watch them. So he let them stop at every flower and follow every lizard, and when a bird sang, he asked, "What is that bird saying?" And he answered, "The bird is saying, 'Hello, beautiful girls.'" With a hand on Rosalie's arm that he hoped she would remember as the consecration of his devotion to his children, Tom gently restrained her to give the girls the lead, to give them all the time in the world.

He helped his daughters undress and stayed with them as they washed their faces and brushed their teeth and said their prayers. The girls relaxed so deeply with him that they asked for Daddy to tell a story instead of Mommy. He invented a character, a prospector who lives in deep tunnels, whose name is a silly sound and the girls meet him by falling down a rabbit hole like Alice's, but not Alice's because this hole leads to a long fall into a special lake, and why is the lake special? Because when a little girl falls into the water and swims to the shore, she comes out dry. And the prospector finds a cave filled with jewels, and the girls bring them home to their mommy and their daddy, who ask them, Where did you get those rubies?

"What happens next?" they wanted to know.

"I'll tell you tomorrow."

Then Tom and Rosalie lay in bed until the silence in the girls' room deepened in the mysterious way that announces how already quiet children have fallen asleep and will not be roused by the muffled sounds of their parents making love.

So Tom and Rosalie brought themselves to each other. Tom used the murder he would commit the next day as a vehicle to bring his grief into the bed, and then he stripped the grief of its selfishness by reminding himself with all his strength that the woman beside him trusted him, and in this true sobriety came mercy and so he was tender.

Three

At the hotel entrance, Tom introduced Debra Seckler to Rosalie, hiding a dizzy bravado, as though he still felt another woman's kiss from a sudden groping in a stairwell. Rosalie said, "I hope we're not invading your vacation by sharing the van with you."

"No, it's nice to meet new people, and the children can play. And this is my husband, Barry." Rosalie took Barry's hand and looked him in the eye, directly, not to look at his stomach.

"Tom," said Tom, offering Barry a hand. "How are you?" He hoped this casual greeting urged the steam away from Seckler's anticipations of more trouble about Alma and the dance.

As the children were introduced, Barry Seckler took Tom aside. "That was awful last night, what I did. It doesn't matter how I thought about it at the time. I would feel the same, I'm sorry."

"As long as you understand," said Tom.

"I do."

"Peace?"

"Life is too short." This was the kind of bullshit homily that Seckler would surely take as the proof of a truce. But Tom would accept no peace. He finished the sentence to himself: I have deferred enough pleasure. Were life really too short, we should all drop our vendettas and sit upon the ground and weep for time wasted in the hunt for pointless retributions. Rather, I say, Life Is Too Long, and regrets can leech the salts from all contentments. Provide against self-torment over the lost opportunity.

...

The driver said his name, but Tom missed it and had to ask Rosalie. Barry said it: "James."

James opened the side door of the white van to let everyone in, and the four children scrambled to the backseats. Perri and Rita, a shy six-year-old, sat together. Tom knew that Perri would have preferred to share the trip with a girl her own age or none at all. Adam, four, sat beside Alma. He was a self-possessed boy with an energetic rasp, the kind of boy Rosalie would talk about later, recalling him with love, his metallic sweaty aroma, the dirt on his neck. She loved boys and their obsessions with ships and machines and war. Tom envied her generosity to the mothers of boys.

The wives took the bench in front of the girls. Who would sit in front? For the insult to Tom's daughter the night before, etiquette obliged Barry's concession to Tom, but the terrible fact of his bloat demanded, for the sake of everyone's comfort, that he take the front seat to avoid spilling his weight on the women.

Tom sat beside Debra. Each wore shorts. Their legs touched. She didn't pull away. So my secret passion reached her, he thought.

As the van left the hotel, Adam looked out at the world in a way the girls would not. They kept their attention within the van while the boy studied a black man cutting the dead fronds of a palm tree. The boy would have been happy watching the man work all day.

"Adam, look at how he uses that machete," said Rosalie. The boy nodded without looking at her.

Between the two front seats was a cooler. James opened it and offered bottles of water and ginger beer. Barry Seckler handed bottles of ginger beer to the adults behind him.

"That's very kind of you," said Rosalie.

"It's a good taste for the tropics," said Debra.

"Yes," said Barry, "because the sweetness hits the tongue first, and then after a few sips, the sharpness of the ginger kind of wakes you up. And then the sugar comes back."

Debra said, "I always liked the idea of bittersweet as a flavor. What is it? Definitions, Barry?"

"Oh, Jesus, bittersweet. Hunh."

"We play this game," said Debra. "We challenge each other to come up with these very ornate definitions for complicated ideas."

"Bittersweet," said Barry. "Okay. There's that balance of the bitter and the sweet, which we use so often to describe an experience of joy that can't be permitted without a retrospective of regret. The damages we have done will always color the pleasures we take. What do you think?"

"It's a B," said Debra.

Rosalie disagreed. "That was really good. Give him an A."

"No," said Barry, "She's right, it's only a B. And I've used the 'retrospective of regret' before."

The van followed the main road along the beach towards the western tip of the island. The misery and the beauty of Jamaica threw up visions at every turn; a fisherman rowed a faded skiff across one side of a bay, towards the rotted stumps of a dead pier, which balanced the composition of the picture, and the whole image seen and then gone too quickly for a photograph; villas behind walls, unfinished.

The van turned left toward the mountains. The road climbed quickly and passed through a breach in the hills, then was swallowed by them, and they were now hidden from the sea, facing higher mountains, distant but not impossibly far.

The children were quiet. The Jamaicans they passed, so dark, looked at the van with suspicion. The parents were not guarded against the repellent implications of their presence on the road, the vacation in someone else's ancestral desolation.

Michael Tolkin

"Tom, what do you do?" asked Debra Seckler.

"I'm a lawyer," he said.

"So am I. Patent litigation. Yourself?"

"This and that. General business. Barry?"

"Lawyer. Mostly on initial public offerings. Rosalie?"

"My father left me some commercial real estate, and I manage the properties. It doesn't take that much time; I have good people working for me so I can be with the children."

"That's very nice," said Barry.

"My mother won't visit the third world," said Debra. "She hates traveling in poor countries because everything has broken down everywhere and she feels helpless."

"But the problem," said Barry, "is that she can't bear their pain, so she turns it against herself."

"Don't we all?" asked Rosalie, warming to the couple, making Tom sick.

"Do we?" asked Tom.

"My mother is a kind of professional skeptic," said Debra.

Barry clapped his hands. "Definitions. Skeptic!"

"Let me try," said Rosalie. "Skeptic. Okay. Here. You take your anxiety over the world, over your powerlessness, and because you don't do enough or can't do enough to save even the little corner of the world that's yours, you doubt everything as a way of giving yourself an alibi for your own weakness. This is skepticism."

"Great," said Barry. "Beautiful."

46

"That's an A+, you just described my mama," said Debra. "If she would only work at a food bank or help with some charity at home, she could travel without feeling so crushed by it."

Barry added, "Maybe she's right. Maybe we shouldn't be here. I'm just another rich American. It costs me nothing to be friendly down here, and the Jamaicans know that if I were sitting on a park bench or waiting at a bus stop at home, and they were to approach me with the same assumption of their affection that I bring to them here, I'd run from them in fear. They hate us. They should."

The road met two other roads in a market town. James pointed to the church behind an iron fence. "That's from the seventeen hundreds." The traffic moved slowly and the van was eyed cautiously, no one gave them a smile. They watched the Jamaicans like something seen from a bathysphere at the bottom of a deep marine trench. They were clumped in slow crowds by the road, forced to sell one another T-shirts imprinted with pictures of motorcycles or Jamaican music stars. Tom felt that their lives were the judgment on the lives of those in the van.

A few minutes past the market town, a thick crowd of Jamaicans filled the road in front of a small church. There were steel drums and flutes, a great noise and excitement.

Barry Seckler asked the driver to stop, and left the van to take a picture.

A boy, Tom guessed seventeen or so, ran past them with a machete, following the parade into the church. Tom wished he had grown up with a religion that admitted violence into its ceremonies.

"What a beautiful thing, all of these people," said Rosalie.

"And the generations are together here, the young and the old," said Debra Seckler.

As the crowd rushed into the church, Tom saw a white man sitting on the steps, knocked over or kicked by someone. He shielded his eyes with one hand to see who was looking at him, then pulled himself to his feet, wrote something in a notebook, and went inside.

The crowd was gone, and the van continued. The scene left a small troubled mark on everyone, even the children.

"Nine Mile," said James. He made a U-turn and pulled off the road beside a high fence topped with coils of razor wire at the foot of a steep driveway. A few other tourist vans were parked at the entrance, and some small cars with rental agency stickers. Five dark men with long dreadlocks stood at the entrance in front of the ticket booth. They wore knit caps with the rasta stripes of green, yellow, and orange. Two of them wore the same T-shirt, a portrait of Haile Selassie as a spiritual warrior in his khaki uniform with an orange band on his cap. The others wore Bob Marley T-shirts, Bob in black and white, with a lazy plume of smoke, green, yellow, and orange, curling from a joint.

"Are these the guides?" Rosalie asked James.

"Don't bother with them," said James.

The first of the Rastas stopped Barry. "You like herb?"

"Not today," said Barry.

"This is herb from Bob Marley plantation."

"Not today."

"Peace, brother," said the Rasta.

Tom bubbled with recklessness. He asked the Rasta, "How many middle-class American tourists with their children beside them buy drugs here?"

"Everyone but you," said the Rasta, without a smile.

The two families passed through the cordon of drug dealers and bought tickets. Inside the gates, an official guide joined them. The families followed him as he explained where they were. They were joined on the tour by a pretty couple from Holland.

"This is where Bob Marley born. Bob Marley born here in 1941."

Barry said to Tom as they walked up the steep hill to the house, "What is it about young Dutch tourists that gives them such an air of annoying holiness? They go around the world with a small backpack, and they're always so calm. The girls are wildly sexy, completely free of guilt, and impossible to seduce."

"You've tried?" asked Tom.

"Well, you know." But Tom didn't know.

At the top of the hill the guide brought them to a small red house with a curtain for a door.

"This is where Bob Marley born. In that building is where Bob Marley buried." The mausoleum was about thirty feet long and twenty feet wide, with high windows and a door inlaid with stained-glass lions.

The guide told everyone to take off their shoes before entering the house. Inside the house, clean small rooms, with no furniture. The guide told them about Bob Marley's mother. "This is where Bob Marley mother make Bob Marley porridge. Are you from Delaware?"

It was an odd question, and they all answered, "No."

"Because Bob Marley mother live in Delaware when Bob Marley nineteen years old, and she call him to Delaware. Bob Marley work in a factory, making cars, before he come back to Jamaica."

Tom tried to imagine Bob Marley as a hidden genius on an American assembly line, and then he wondered what cars were made in Delaware. Perhaps the guide meant Bob Marley had lived in Detroit.

Perri didn't know why they were there or what this was for. Tom tried to explain. "Bob Marley was a great musician. The Jamaicans are poor people, and he sang about their lives. His music touched them, and it touched the world. That's the power of music."

The girls listened deafly. They were fascinated by the small house.

"Did the whole family live here?" asked Perri.

"Yes," said the guide.

Tom was embarrassed by his daughter's question. It reflects badly on me, he thought.

On the light green walls, the pilgrims had left their offerings: postcards, reverential graffiti in all the languages of the world, cigarette papers, flowers. There was nothing to see once you'd seen it for a few minutes, nothing to study except your own attempt to draw deeper significance from the place. The stoned docent with his thick braids gave few clues to his own character, and Tom, for lack of any other subject, wondered about him. How much did he make in a week?

"This is the rock what Bob Marley sat on when he wrote 'Positive Vibrations.'"

The view was ridiculous, perfect in every detail physically and morally. If a song should come from any place, then let it come from here, on a mountain whose peak is hidden in the clouds behind you. The sound of a hammer hitting a board somewhere down the hill, the clucking of chickens, a radio with the news, a man shouting for help with a heavy box, the heat, the wet air filled with the resins of small fires in crude stoves, the repulsion Tom felt for Barry Seckler, who made Alma dance like a whore; it was impossible not to be completely there, distractions overwhelmed by the thick waters of life, assembled as a rebus Tom could not decipher. Tom wanted to ask Barry Seckler, Who allegorized you into my life?

Inside the mausoleum, the shock of the tomb's dignity made them quiet. The marble sarcophagus was eight feet high. The guide told them that the stone was a gift from the Italian government and that the stained-glass windows came from Ethiopia. African instruments, primitive guitars and tribal drums, hung on the wall, none of them grand enough for the occasion. Something larger than a songwriter was buried or remembered here. Barry tapped Tom's arm and nodded to the Dutch girl, who had settled a joint on the base of the sarcophagus as an offering.

Barry whispered, "Here's a definition of the Dutch. They roam the hip shrines of the world and then return to the Netherlands and Scandinavia with their thinness, their frugality, their lack of humor, their aura of sanctity, their affability with the natives, their Charles Mingus tapes, to disappear into their smoky cafés and jazz clubs, huddled in philosophical conversations, and what had impressed us, had threatened us, their independence, their detachment from the disturbances of traveling with so little money, becomes, when you look closely at their lives at home, indifference. Mark this, the flip side of Dutch tolerance is Dutch indifference."

"Bob Marley is a holy man," said the guide. "He bring the world together."

They left. Tom tipped the guide. The Dutch couple also gave money. Maybe they're not so bad, thought Tom. It was all Seckler's view of them.

In the van, Debra asked, "Do you think Bob Marley really did bring the world together?"

"Is the world together?" asked her husband.

Rosalie raised her hand with too much bright excitement, annoying Tom. "He did give some poor people hope. That's worth something," she said.

"It's not an illusion?" asked Debra.

"I don't think so," said Rosalie.

Nine Mile was at the top of the hill, and from there to the main road taking them to the coast, they listened to music. Debra's cute leg rolled into Tom's, and instead of shifting his leg out of courtesy, he pressed back. Her skin was slippery with sweat, and this conducted, so he wanted to believe, a special charge. If this was the closest he might come to cuckolding Barry Seckler, he would take full pleasure and force Debra to pull away or play the game, to be conscious of the touch. What would Rosalie see if she looked at them? She might see nothing, the contact was so slight.

The van bumped across muddy ruts where the rains had sluiced through the pavement. "The road gets worse before it gets better," said James.

Tom considered James's simple sentence as the fortune cookie of his day. Do I have to read all of this as a parable of something within me? The road of life? I'm a muddy green island inhabited by the poor descendants of slaves. And the road of my life takes me from hilltop shrines to wherever we are now, let me see how I can conjure this place appropriately, to . . . to barren fields . . . to old farms abandoned by their tenants and left to seed?

They drove past farm or plantation fields filled with tall grass and young trees.

Tom thought: Some part of me is just like this? But some part of me is just like some part of every part of the universe.

And if the muddy road was how he felt, ahead was the highway, and from the way the fields rolled downhill to another dense grove, a sense that beyond all of this land the ocean was near, and so the waterfalls were near, and with them finally the place where he would kill Barry Seckler.

Tom stopped trying to think of things to say. The vacation was a ruin already. The children and his wife were having a fine old time. His wife probably thought that the sun and the warm water and the visions released by Jamaica succored Tom's need for profound revelation.

I was a criminal because I needed a story in my life, thought Tom. My secret crimes made me important. The secret made me arrogant, but that private disdain subsidized my occasional benevolence.

The soft leg against his. Nothing to add to that. Even at the moment, the leg's pressure belonged to the past, to what he had wanted, not what he felt now. His desire for her was dimming, dimming, gone. Just this touch was wrong, wrong to his wife, wrong to Debra Seckler, wrong for his children in the backseat. How could he make love to another man's wife with all of their children so close? He pulled his leg away. Their skin had bonded, and the separation, which he advanced slowly, ran between them, the lazy end of a long and funny kiss. For the first time in all their bumping together, he felt her erotic consciousness rising into her skin. This made him even unhappier. He wanted to tell Barry that all that needed mending was the direction of his apology, which belonged not to Tom but to Alma. But how do you apologize to a little girl for an insult when the explanation of the offense would constitute another violation?

If there was no apology, there was only revenge. The road, representing to Tom that part of him which always descended from glorious mountaintop slum to beachside tourism, settled into the final easy grade to the coastal plain. What would this mean as a spiritual paradigm, he wondered. Signs for restaurants and hotels, nothing so awfully polished as the advertising in America; hand-painted and charming for the pitiful hopes squeezed within the crude caricatures of happy tourists and happy Jamaicans. And then everywhere around them something green, a field, a big tree, and then the ocean, always a challenge for purpose. How to read this now? James made a left turn off the coast road and up a hill into the parking lot for Dunn's River Falls, and into a line of tour buses from the big hotels and cruise ships. Tom understood the scene around him immediately: no entrance to the falls without first navigating the hundred stalls of bad crafts, the carvings of long-necked African queens, the jute handbags, and everywhere T-shirts of Bob Marley. James opened the van's door, and Tom helped his children out. He was happy to hoist them both from the van to the ground, a feeling of solid merit for giving them a lift into the air above him and bringing their faces close to his.

"You have to get special shoes for climbing the falls," said James. "The falls are slippery." Jamaicans in booths offered neoprene felt-soled boots for rent.

Debra put on her boots and said to Barry, "How do you define these? The world gives us so many experiences that are impossible to describe. Was it always this way?"

"Definition?" asked Barry. "You say, 'A knight in armor on a black horse.' Everyone gets that. You say, 'A man in neoprene boots with felt soles for traction on wet rocks.' Who understands that? So many words to define a thing, the name is a process. Who gets it? I have them on, and I don't get it. Maybe that's why we have so much music in our lives now, so many forms and melodies. The man who first said, 'A knight on a black horse,' how many songs did he know? How many melodies? How many forms of music? The man who says 'neoprene boots' is a prisoner. He is speechless. The only language to contain his experience is music."

The parking lot was at the top of the falls. From the ticket booth they walked down a winding trail, away from the falls to the beach, where they fell in line with a busload from a hotel in Ocho Rios. A guide introduced himself.

"I am Lyall, and I am your guide today. We are all going to have fun, and we are all going to have a safe trip. I only lose people on Tuesdays, and today is Wednesday." This brought a laugh to those who thought it was funny. Some of the tourists carried video cameras in waterproof cases.

Lyall explained the rules. Everyone would hold hands going up the falls. Whoever wanted a video record of the trip could pay for it now, and at the top of the falls a copy would be waiting, or you could hire someone to take a movie with the camera you brought. The camera would be safe. Lyall took the hand of the first person in line, an older woman. She in turn held her husband's hand, and he held the hand of a pretty teenager who held the hand of her brother, who held his father's hand, and his father led Tom, who led Alma who led Rosalie who led Perri who led Debra who led Adam who led Rita who led Barry and after that Tom didn't care.

They left the sand and stepped up on the rocks. Fresh cold water filled their boots, but the felt soles gave traction. The climb brought to Tom a feeling of increased competence. The group stopped in a wide pool. Above them, a thousand tourists held hands in a line, up the ladder of falls and pools, on steps carved along the side. Tom looked back. The bottom of the falls was lost around a bend, but through the trees, he saw the blue bay and two rotting fishing boats lying at anchor. The thread of humanity extruding from the beach suggested a hatchery releasing its fry.

Couples posed and mugged for the photographers and the men with the video cameras. Children jumped into a deep hole in the pool. Others brought themselves to the wide curtain of water falling from the ledge above, put their arms into the veil, parting the water on a seam, and then stepped through to a cave behind.

Lyall called for the next ascent.

Tom changed his place in the line and allowed Barry to lead him.

The line began slowly.

Here the falls were steep.

There was none of the bonhomie of the first pitch, none of that hospitality, none of those free-flowing condolences for the little slips along the way, none of the hands extended when the line broke. This part of the climb scared them.

Mothers complained to Lyall about the danger of the climb. Lyall said it was safe. "Look up, everyone has made it. You don't see any bodies in the water."

Tom held Barry's hand. "I don't feel well," said Seckler. "This isn't fun for me right now."

His distress alarmed Tom. He wanted to kill Seckler, not watch him drop dead of a heart attack, and he wanted to face him. Tom could have pulled Seckler's arm and yanked him off the steps, but the fall wouldn't kill him. Seckler held Tom's left hand, and Tom switched to his right because the rock he needed for a hold was too slick, and a solid tree root above it offered a better grip. Once he secured a hold on the root, the waterfall and rocks seemed to reverse energy, and where everything until that moment pulled him towards the beach, now the buoyant pleasure of the danger pushed Tom upwards to the next ledge, without effort, as though Barry Seckler found Tom no more trouble than an old suitcase.

The worst of it behind them, the group pulled themselves with triumphant smiles to a broad shallow pool.

Tom looked up. The next section was a long stairway with an iron rail. It will have to be now, thought

Tom, at the center of the pool's edge, looking down a forty-foot drop.

Rosalie splashed water at the girls. Tom picked them up under each arm and carried them squealing around the rocks, where a clump of twenty or so tourists waited their turn to walk into a cave behind another waterfall. The little chamber could hold five people. Tom waited with the girls. Instead of walking around the waterfall, he carried them through it, but this fall was heavier than the one below, and the force of the water knocked them over. Alma went under. Tom held her arm and brought her back to the air. She refused to cry. In the water and the sun, by the love of her father and a contempt for public shame, she willed in herself the rudiments of courage. She would not give to anyone the entertainment of her tender sobbing. He loved her for this.

Rosalie asked them to pose for a picture. The snapshot is on a wall somewhere, even today; Tom between his daughters, leaning over to fit the frame.

Tom then let go of the girls and walked to the ledge. Barry Seckler kicked through the water and stood beside him, certain that the castigation of the night before, in his view justifiable though unnecessary, was over, and that the trip today had brought the men into a friendship that might last. Tom said to him, "What you did to my daughter."

"What?" asked Seckler, who looked hard into Tom's eyes, seeing, Tom was sure, how sad and remote they were, and then how dangerous.

Tom mumbled, "What you did to my daughter. You should not have made her dance."

"I thought we were over this."

"No."

"Come on, man, it was a mistake. I told you that. She's fine. Look at her."

Tom put a hand on Seckler's arm. Seckler now saw in his eyes the mournful resolve of an error gone too far for restoration. Tom thought, I can die here. This can kill me, too.

Tom pushed Seckler to the edge. Tom had the advantage; his foot was braced against a rock, and Seckler was slipping in the swift-moving water.

"Don't do this," said Barry.

"What?"

"I think you want to kill me."

"I don't know what else to do."

"I can help you."

"It's too late."

Seckler cried out, "Help! He's killing me! Help me!" He sounded like what he was, a man about to die, a man frightened for his life, a child.

"This is for my daughter," said Tom.

Later, someone would say that from the next step up the falls, the two men looked like friends having fun; what had been desperate was seen as exuberant pleasure.

Barry Seckler dropped forty feet, breaking open his head. As he fell, everyone watching heard his anguish, the agonal cry of a man knowing that at the end of this, his children would lose their father.

Debra Seckler grabbed her children and pushed them away from the edge. In fractions of seconds, up and down the line of tourists, the word went out that something terrible had happened.

Rosalie, Alma, and Perri saw what happened. They had never seen Tom fight before.

It was understood that this was a murder and not an accident.

There he was, dead in the water. The difficult climb up the rocks from that pool was harder going down. Debra could not find a hold, and kind people lifted her away from the rocks and lowered her, passing her along from hand to hand. Those who touched her would remember their meticulous intention, only to help her, and the reward of a sensation of intense honesty.

Barry was face down. Debra, beside him, asked for help, and from a watchful crowd of young Jamaican men, two stepped forward, and then all, and they turned him over. The cracked side of his head seeped blood. She lifted his head out of the water and cupped a hand and washed the wound with water. She looked up and met Tom's eyes. Tom was surrounded by Jamaicans and tourists.

She kissed her fat dead husband's lips, and cried to him, and sang. Tom couldn't hear the song over the water.

Tom hated everything, the sullen beauty of the falls, the easy way that the tropics delivered clarity. Tom thought: I never understood the world until now. I never understood the danger of evil until now.

I was a good man who did one thing wrong. Then he thought, More than one.

...

Children cried, "Daddy!" The voices of his daughters, the voices of Rita and Adam Seckler, who were in the lower pool. Tom leaned over the edge of the cliff to get a better view, but then the men crowding around him pulled him away, fearing that he would jump.

I won't jump, he could have told them, but who would have believed him, and why be reasonable now? He could toss them an apology like a chunk of meat, watch the apology rise and fall on a parabola of their anticipation and then disappointment at such a meager offering. Better to stay silent and keep them entertained by their fantasies of what he should or might do now that they had him on the way to prison.

All of this happened at once: James the driver was called by the river guides. James brought a woman from the ticket booth who gently coached the Seckler children away from the body and led them to the side of the river, where others lifted them out of the water. There was a policeman in the water, his pants rolled up, and someone gave him a video camera. The policeman, and others, watched the playback on the camera's screen, and Tom understood that they were looking at him pushing

Barry Seckler to his death. At the same time, Rosalie, with the girls beside her, cried out, "Why, Tom, why?"

This delighted the crowd. A voice from the hill added in mockery, "Why, Tom, why?"

The people around him also wanted to know. "Why did you push that man, sir?"

"I'm sorry," Tom said again. It was too complicated. He might have said, "He made my daughter dance. He asked my daughter to dance, and who knows when the degradation of what happened to her will work its way into action? Should I wait thirty years, and if she turns into a junkie, should I track him down and kill him then? You don't know that she wasn't ruined by what happened last night." But he couldn't say this. It wasn't the knight in armor on the horse. It was neoprene boots with felt soles. It was the video camera with the thing on the side where you look at the picture. The thing, the little screen, and bad sound. The viewing-screen thing. That's what it was.

The crowd's sound lost its definition. The men guarding Tom opened a breach in their wall around him to let the police through. The men closest to Tom took his hands and pulled on his arms, as though a white man in a bathing suit could be dangerous.

But I am dangerous, thought Tom. I just killed a man. This thought impressed itself heavily with the advent of the police, dropping Tom to his knees, and the men around him yanked him to his feet. He dropped again, hurting his knees on the rocks in the cold water.

I'm scared, thought Tom. I am now frightened to death. I have never been so scared of anything in my life. And I am making a fool of myself in front of the policemen. In America, the police would have asked the men holding Tom to let him go. They would have threatened the volunteer guards with nightsticks, but this was not America, Tom knew that, this was a place where a crowd could hold a man and hurt him, pull his arms hard when he falls to his knees, and the police would allow it. Klaxons sounded. Tom liked the two-note call, it reminded him of movies with the French resistance and the alarm made when the gestapo arrives. In movies, the message of the Klaxon is death. In Jamaica, this Klaxon brought an ambulance and a gurney, and the men who rolled Barry Seckler's enormous body onto a stretcher. They couldn't expect the stretcher to hold his weight, but it helped. Four men to each side, floating him into deeper water, where they could slip the litter beneath him. Tom would have liked to watch the rest of the effort, but he was taken away to the riverbank.

"What is your name?" a policeman asked him.

"Tom Levy."

"And where are you from?"

"America."

"And where are you staying in Jamaica?"

"The Montego House."

"These people say that you pushed that man over the falls. I saw the videotape. It looks as though you did. Can you tell me what happened?"

"I'd like to speak to a lawyer."

"Last night at the Montego House, you had a bad word with this man. Why? What happened last night, Mr. Levy?"

"He made advances at my daughter."

"Could you explain what you mean?"

"He made my daughter dance."

"Did he touch your daughter?"

"He made her dance like a whore."

...

Rosalie stood alone in the water with Perri and Alma. No one was helping them. Somewhere, someone gave relief to Debra Seckler and her two children, but no one there even knew that the killer's wife watched the arrest of her husband.

The police pulled Tom to the hillside, where the crowd had flattened the bushes and grasses. His feet slipped, and he fell on his face. He was covered in mud, he was filthy, and the police were filthy, too, and mad about it. Tom saw Rosalie. "Rosalie, Rosalie, I'm sorry."

She kept moving with the girls and would not look back, she would not let him turn her into a pillar of salt. Little Alma looked back, and so did Perri. He would have raised a hand to let them draw comfort and hope from a confident gesture, but his arms were bound.

The police lifted Tom and handed him up the hill to more Jamaicans, the poor men who wanted only to work, and even this unpaid labor answered their needs for effort with purpose. Tom gave himself to the men who lifted him, and let his body help them by now holding a leg stiff, now tilting his head away so a hand could better wrap around the back of his neck.

Fog over everything. Too much pleasure in the obscurity of the day. This is what I asked for. This is what I came here to do. I have erased so much of my life that I am blind. There is only the rushing sound of the waterfalls, which could be just the sound of the blood in my ears. There is temperature, the afternoon heat, with a pledge of rain, with a thin slice of electricity in the taste of the air. There is gravity, because I am not floating away. But there is nothing to see.

The police pushed Tom into the backseat of a car.

"Open your eyes, please, sir," said one of them.

Tom obliged. It made no difference. His eyes worked but to no purpose. All of his opinions, theories, and field notes, the murky half-toned ideas that float on the periphery of language, all of this rushed away from him, chased off the property by a barking horde of mistakes. He saw road and trees and the sea between the trees and past the road, and the romance and pity of the place meant nothing, either version of the island equally valid and equally pointless.

At the Ocho Rios police station, they gave him dry clothing, a blue prison shirt and blue pants. He was put into a cell, alone.

A new man came into his life, shining, dark, confident, with merry eyes, a man of patience and authority. "I am Captain Dekker of the police."

"Tom Levy."

"Well, well, well, Mr. Levy. So you have a fight in the falls, and the man dies. You pushed him, and we have this on videotape. What were you thinking, Mr. Levy?"

"I made a mistake."

"Yes you did."

"No. No, no, no, no, no. I should have killed the singer."

...

Seven months later, Tom Levy was in prison in Kingston, sentenced for the rest of his life.

The trial was short, nine days. His parents sat behind him in the courtroom and paid his lawyer well, but Tom offered no defense.

His family came for a last visit when the trial was over, Rosalie with the girls and his mother and father and his sister. He was allowed to hug them. No one could say anything that made sense. His mother and father, who had once been so specific, spoke to him in generic bromides. "Why, Tom, why?" But what else could they say? As he stood there, answering, "I don't know," not wanting to explain himself anymore, he stared at them and forgot what they looked like.

His sister spoke to him privately. "You don't know the damage that you've done. I couldn't even tell you what I feel. The world has exhausted all analogies."

"You could try."

"No."

"It might be a kindness. I need charity."

"No. You need to say that you need charity. Charity, for you, Tom, is another bead in your chain of little strategies. I've been watching you since you were five. You, Tom, are an undercover agent."

"And who runs me?"

"I did not call you a spy, because spies are powerless messengers, single-purpose demons or angels turned on and off as the need for them requires."

"Undercover with what agency of what government?"

"The world of crime. You're an ambassador from the world of crime."

"Undercover agent or ambassador?"

"Did I say ambassador?"

"Yes."

"Then, Tom, I'll stay with both opinions, agent and ambassador together. The agent hides while the ambassador enters through the front door, and the agent leaves without turning his back. He can never reveal his true purpose. The ambassador presents his papers. You're the assassin who got caught. You're on trial for the murder of a man you didn't know."

"I knew him."

"This murder was not your first evil deed. I saw you falling into crime when you were a little boy. It hurt you more not to steal than it hurt the other boys. You wanted to steal money from Mom's purse, rubbers from Dad's drawers."

"How did you know?"

"Moses killed an Egyptian. It says in the Bible that he saw an Egyptian beating up a Hebrew, and when he looked this way and that and saw no one, then he killed the Egyptian. Sometime later he found two Hebrew slaves fighting, and he told them to stop, and they said, 'What are you going to do? Are you going to kill us the way you killed the Egyptian?' You didn't know I was watching, but I was there. I know you."

"Will you look after Rosalie and the girls?"

"Of course I will. I love them. I'm going to spend as much time with the girls as I can, and I'm going to do right by this side of the family. I'm going to help Rosalie make a new life, help her find a job, and find a good father for the girls."

...

During the trial, remanded to the district's small jail, protected, a little, by his American passport but knowing that prison was certain, Tom looked hopefully, even eagerly, ahead to an ecstatic boredom, a concentration of misery made enlightening as the resolving experience of his life. After three months in the Spanish Town Prison, around the bay from Kingston, to his surprise and disappointment, the day of his sentencing was not, he feared, and never would be, the division between before and after. Prison, in the beginning, was just the next place he went to after the place he had been before. Some days were good, some days were bad.

The Spanish Town Prison was hell, of course, a universe of pain and insult, six thousand men behind stone walls whose foundations were older than Boston. Someone was always screaming somewhere. Gang wars from outside continued inside, and the guards bet among themselves on fights that ended in death. Tom, hating himself, stifled his impulse to indignation, the voice of the American who might say, "I have my rights." He wanted no rights beyond those he could earn.

But he did want something, he wanted the approval of the brutal men around him. They ignored him. Scarred, vicious men passed him without notice. He had killed a man to protect his daughter's honor, everyone understood this. He wasn't in prison because in a drunken coma he had run his car into three Jamaican children, or been caught transporting drugs. His crime was human.

As they avoided him, he decided that his intimidating aura of tragedy demanded from others a cautious and distant veneration.

Or so he thought at first.

After a time, he saw their opinion of him as nothing more than cold indifference.

And then he knew that he was wrong, they were offering friendship all the time, in their own way, and that they were all strangers to one another.

Now he embarrassed himself for wanting validation from such poor men. He knew he was confused, that he had wanted respect, yet he pushed these men away and created their disdain.

Looking back on his life, Tom saw a pattern, of first imagining that his worst feelings were the general opinion, the worst feelings about himself or others, and then sharing those opinions with people more generous to the world who pushed him away, not wanting to be stained.

Tom wanted to dig through the junk heap of his life until he found the layer where he had lost attachment to those scraps of his character that could summon worthy regard. He knew that if he could only pull the conflicts together, he would rescue himself from the whole flotilla of misjudgments that ended with a dead fat man at the bottom of a waterfall. He wanted this, he wanted to fix himself, but to what end? He was here for the rest of his life. What good if this enlightened vision of himself finally arrived?

Slowly, Tom made friends. If someone needed help moving a bed, Tom was there to give a hand. If someone needed help reading a brief from his lawyer, Tom was there. The thanks he received made him grieve more deeply for the time he had wasted.

He understood this: If I could have recognized true friendship when offered, throughout my life, I would not be the person I am, and therefore I would not be here. Much earlier in life I would have joined in friendship with strong good people, men and women, not my gang of sleazy scammers, and we would have helped one another.

He imagined the contours of such help. It would have the energetic zest of his conspiracy without the cynicism, that suspicion of everyone else. He would make more money, but it might take longer, and his friends would always be there to point out new opportunities.

He lay on the floor of his cell, his arms crossed over his chest, their weight the two soft heads of his little girls stretched out on the floor beside him, in the living room of a condominium they rented at a ski resort in Vermont, watching the logs spark in the fireplace.

Skiing, yes, they would go skiing all winter long. His good friends and their families would rent condominiums in the same place, and they would all gather together at the end of the day and make dinner, big pots of spaghetti and huge salads made of nothing but iceberg lettuce. Rosalie never bought iceberg lettuce because it lacked the vitamin content of romaine, but children love iceberg's noisy crunch, especially with sweet creamy dressing from a bottle. They eat large bags of potato chips, forbidden at home, but what the hell, right? It's a vacation. Let's relax. One of his friends is sure to know something about wine, and he brings a dozen different bottles, and all of them are good.

After dinner they play Scrabble together and let the children win, not that the children aren't all bright and capable, and so intellectually elastic that they make wonderful words on their own.

They rent videos that everyone can watch. One of the fathers rents Jimmy Cliff in *The Harder They Come*, a film about a poor Jamaican singer who turns to crime and is shot to death in a mangrove swamp. With the first reggae song, the little girls are moved to stand in front of the television and dance, shaken by the music out of their bodies and their modesty, but they don't want to dance, the music captures them, invisible strings reach out and jerk them like marionettes, and they cry out for help, and then Tom reaches for his machine gun and shoots the television, and then every television in the ski resort, and then he shoots everyone who threatens his children, all the children, and he goes on shooting.

...

His father died after Tom's ninth month in prison, and his mother died soon after.

Rosalie visited without the children to bring him the news. She came with a white Jamaican lawyer. She wore a pretty yellow sundress and white sandals.

"Yesterday, after I left, your sister told the girls that you were dead. She told the girls that I had gone to Jamaica to identify your body. She told them that Jamaican law calls for your cremation. I know it's horrible, but we want to make a hard boundary between the day you killed Barry Seckler and their future. I couldn't tell them the story and look them in the eyes. When I come back, I'll give them the comfort that I can."

"What did I die of?"

"We said you had a heart attack. We didn't want you to be murdered. A heart attack was easy. We'll have a memorial service when I go home."

"What will you say at the funeral?"

"We'll talk about the man we remember, the man we loved. It will be wonderful for the girls and wonderful for me. We'll laugh about you. We'll remember your many kindnesses. The official story now is that you went crazy on your vacation and started to fight someone, and something terrible happened. Perhaps you had a fever. We all agree not to dwell on what you did or why. You were found guilty of murder in Jamaica, while in America you might have been convicted of manslaughter. The prison conditions were hard, you were delicate, and you died. Each of the girls has a therapist who is helping her to remember you with love. Sign here."

Tom signed. "Have you had any contact with Debra Seckler?"

"Yes. When you were sentenced."

"Will you tell her I'm dead?"

"Yes."

"I could write to the girls. I could send them mail. I can tell them I'm alive."

"You won't."

"How do you know?"

"Because you don't want to hurt them any more than you have."

"I may get out someday."

"No. You're here forever, which won't be long. You'll get old in here fast, and you'll get sick in here, and you will die in here. I'm sorry, I hope you believe that I'm sorry."

They shook hands. Then she kissed him on the cheek. "We were having such a lovely day. They were lovely people."

Four

One morning, Tom looked in the mirror and saw a man with a white beard that fell to his chest, and white hair below his shoulders. The man had eyes set deep in hollow sockets. The beard was thick, but what he could see of the man's cheeks was furrowed. The white-haired man's nose had a high bridge that twisted to the right and then flattened.

Tom touched the nose.

This is me, he thought.

He knew this, years had gone by. The last thing I remember was a visit from my wife. I have been in a fight, or I have fallen, or been pushed. My memory dissolved, but I'm back into myself, and I remember who I was before I grew this beard. I am Tom Levy, and I killed a man.

There were four iron cots in the cell. A black man, perhaps thirty, smoked a cigarette and looked up at him with little curiosity. Tom, careful not to make eye contact in the mirror, wanted to stay suspended in the peace of his recovered self without announcing his return to consciousness. He needed time to make sense of things.

What if I've been a zombie for twenty years? What if this man and others feed me, dress me, wash me? Have I been silent for twenty years? Do I talk, but without consciousness of my speech? And if I speak, what do I speak? Have I learned the Jamaican patois?

What if I have been a savage man, fighting and stabbing? What if I am cruel and a leader? What if this man protects me? What if this man is my prison lover?

Tom lifted his shirt. He was well muscled, and his chest was covered in old scars. And were these hands his, so burned and calloused? How did this happen?

Tom cleared his throat. The man on the cot said nothing. Well, a man clears his throat, no matter who he is or what.

The smells of the prison rushed at Tom like a sound, like music. The heavy tropical air carried the rich brew of a harbor, and the close relish of cooking oil, wood smoke, and a sewer, like a bass, supporting all the vibrations of stink, and as each scent tickled Tom's attention, it came with an emotion: the smoke was distant lust, the aroma of cooking was disgust, the feeling from the sewer was a paradox of repulsion and love.

He studied the mirror. I would not know this was me except that I know my name.

Those dark steady eyes are my eyes, which used to be even and dull, practiced in their steady focus. My face records the triumph of repentance over still visible and unmistakable traces of the depravity of that dullness. I am beautiful! My panic is gone!

He touched his nose. Someone hit me.

I was in a fight. I will not assume that the punch that might have knocked me into years of insensibility is proof of defeat. I may have won. And I have been, for years, so completely within the routines of my penance that time dissolved and, with time, my crime.

How many years?

Something in me stands corrected. I look like a saint.

Beneath the mirror was a washbasin. Tom ran the water and splashed it on his face. This must be why I was standing here. I was here to wash my face. Behind him, in the mirror, Tom watched the smoker on the bed. It was time to learn more.

"Where do I get a shave?" Tom asked.

The man on the cot smiled at him, like a father in love with a baby. "What?"

"Where do I get a shave around here?"

"I'll be right back." The man ran from the room, shouting down the corridor, "He spoke! He spoke! He wants a shave! Levy wants a shave! Levy wants a shave! He spoke!"

A hundred prisoners gathered outside the cell. Tom watched them, remembering some of their faces from his first year in the prison. There were two white men among them.

"Can someone tell me my story?" Tom asked, keeping his eyes averted from the white men, who Tom supposed were drug dealers, so the blacks would not feel divided from his respect. "Can someone tell me how I broke my nose and why my hair is white?" Tom's voice was as unfamiliar to him as his face, lower, softer, not so aggressively placed in the middle register, not so tight. He liked this new voice. "Can someone tell me how long I have been here? Have I been well? Have I been a burden or of service? Please, how long have I been here?"

The first man to answer was the man from his cell. "Seven years."

"And my hair turned white in seven years?"

"Yes."

"And how did I break my nose?"

An old man in the crowd started to answer, excitedly, but he spoke an impossibly difficult argot, and Tom could understand none of it. One of the white men, an American, saw Tom's distress. "I'll help you," he said. "I know what he's saying." So the old man explained, and the American translated.

"When you came into the jail, you knew nobody. For the first year, everyone asked about you, what you had done. You were the man who killed a tourist who had offended your daughter. Everyone knew the story. No one blamed you."

"But I shouldn't have done it."

"No one blamed you. Still, this is prison, and men challenged your honor. A thief from Negril asked you to fight. You had no choice. He hit you, and you hit him. He hit you in the face, with a rock he kept hidden, and you fell. You were taken to the infirmary. There was a condemned man in the bed next to yours who took you for an angel. He had been tortured for days by the guards. His hanging was due in a week, and the warden wanted the man presentable because the execution would be observed by the press.

"The condemned man told you a story. He was seen talking to you every day, all day and all night, for his final seven days. You asked him questions at first, and he answered, but then you stopped asking questions and you listened. The condemned man whispered to you.

"And all the time that he talked, your hair lost its color. On the day he finished, they came for him and walked him to the gallows. And on that day, your hair finished turning the color it is today, that terrifying white. And since that day, silence has been your companion. You have walked among us, eating, dressing, bathing, never saying a word, minding yourself. We spoke to you, but you never answered."

"What did the hanged man tell me?"

"Only you know the story. We have been waiting for it."

"I don't remember it. I don't even remember the hanged man."

"You must remember!" The old man jumped at him and grabbed his shoulders. "You were told a story that cannot fit inside you without coming out. Someone else's memory resides inside of you, it was placed there by a man who was hanged, perhaps because of the story, and he was desperate to keep the story alive. Why? His mystery is crawling inside of you, looking for a way over the wall.

The story the hanged man told you is inside you like all of us are inside of this prison. And if you tell us that story, you will free yourself, and those who hear the story will also be free."

Tom asked, "How?"

"What do you remember?"

"About what?"

"Everything. Tell us your life story. Tell us everything you know."

The need to help these men met the fear that he would fail them and be hated by them for the rest of his life in this prison. He had no memory of the hanged man, no memory of the fight. Tom wanted to throw up, but then the menacing sickness and fear he felt from this flashed in his soul like lightning, exposing the shape of the story. Then the fear subsided into confusion, and he lost sight of the thing the hanged man had placed there.

"I need to sit down."

"Do you remember something?" someone asked.

"Maybe. I saw something, but it disappeared."

Word of Tom's recovery spread through the prison. The crowd outside his cell grew larger.

A guard with epaulets and a chevron on his white sleeve asked Tom his name.

"Tom Levy."

"And do you need a doctor?"

"No," said Tom. "I'm fine."

"Why did you not speak for so long?"

Tom looked the man in the eye and knew how to win some time for himself. He answered with a smile, "I had nothing to say."

The guard laughed, and then everyone laughed, not for long but in relief. There would be no investigation, no interruption, Tom would stay in the cell.

The guard told the men to clear the corridor.

I owe these men. They have protected me during my deep trance.

In losing his body, he had gained the astral, with an immediacy so complete that for seven years he knew time as a single instant with no voluptuous surges advancing and retreating, so nothing to gauge position, so no reflection, so no memory. How to explain his triumphant return to the shattered world? Something rescued him, but what, or who?

"I want to help you," said Tom. "Where do I begin?"

"Tell us the story of your life."

"Why?"

"To protect his message against its enemies, the hanged man wove his story into you. As you tell your own story, we will find that knot among the threads of your life. You might remember an ordinary moment, a moment of no obvious consequence to you, when without warning you will begin to tell a story you could not possibly have lived."

"Then I'll start with the story of the murder, because nothing else in my life was ever so exciting or coherent," said Tom.

And so he did, as best as he could. He told them about the hotel, and the people there, and the sour mood of his week, and he told them about his daughters, how much he loved them, how beautiful and true they were, how he disdained to call them special, to give them any higher worth. He remembered Perri's warm damp hand, and Alma's cool grip, the night he walked with them, the night before the murder.

He told his prison mates about the band, and about the singer's tawdry pleasure in dancing with a four-year-old. He told them about Barry Seckler, and the trip to Nine Mile, and the struggle in the waterfall, and the blood. He told them about the last visit with his wife, and then he told them of the early days in the prison. He told them the story of Paul Farrar and his conspiracy of educated professionals.

It was an interesting story, and he told it honestly. It was certainly filled with more drama than any of the stories he might have heard at his high school reunion, but every man around him could tell stories of violence. He saw how they listened with full attention, because their lives depended on him. He related each detail simply, trying to press the redeeming angel's oil of sanctification from every word. When he paused for breath, or a sip of water, he waited with his audience for truth to fill the room, for the twinkling instant of boundless change.

He finished the story up to the beginning of telling this story.

"So I was asked to tell the story of the murder and what I remember of everything that followed. Now I'm in prison in Jamaica, telling you a story, and I've reached the end. I'm sorry," said Tom. "It's not there."

"It is there," said the old man, "and you have only begun. None of us is going anywhere quickly. When the time comes, you'll call us together."

It was morning. Tom followed these friends, old to his life but new to his awareness, to the prison mess hall. Tom marveled that he had survived for so long in his trance, walking these gloomy halls. His escort led him to a table where other prisoners, having already heard the news of his awakening, urged a share of their food on him, hoping, by selfish kindness, to provoke the hanged man's legend from its living tomb.

The guards, for whom Tom's trance had advanced him, over the years, towards invisibility, saw him chatting and laughing with the crowd at the table and promptly put him in a cell, alone. They feared nothing but any sudden difference in the air, and Tom's new state of being scared them like a hurricane.

The cell was wet and dark. There were rats in the corner, and large bugs, which he could feel as they crawled over him, but none of this bothered him, because he was thinking about the missionary, and Phineas. He wondered if someone had ever printed Yael's photographs. Were the pictures fine enough for the book she dreamed of? If there were good pictures of the orgies, he supposed so. There was a market for artful sex books.

What would her friends do with that picture of the church garden?

Tom called out, "Can anyone hear me?"

There was a voice from the cell next to his. "Yes, I can hear you."

"I just remembered something that never happened to me."

"A dream?"

"No. I have a story to tell. The men in my cell block are waiting for it."

"Tell me and I will pass it along. There is a pipe in my cell. It carries my voice."

"Tell them I remember what the hanged man told me."

Word was passed along the corridor for everyone nearby to be quiet. A wave of silence moved through the prison until the only sound was of the guards' batons ringing the bars of the cells, because the quiet made them nervous.

"A few years ago," Tom began, "an American missionary came to rebuild the church in a Jamaican hill town, so remote that some of the villagers had never seen the ocean. The missionary wrote a letter to his bishop. . . ."

. . .

"They are extraordinarily skillful in using their hands, and they have a fantastic and I think impeccable visual taste, considering their poverty and the poverty of their materials, but their faith and intellectual notions are archaic in the extreme. They find it difficult or impossible to grasp the general concepts that might lead to their liberation. They have little sense of cumulative, as opposed to repetitive, time, and they cloud their history with Rastafarian fantasies that Haile Selassie was the messiah. So the notion of progress, I should say linear progress, is incomprehensible to them. Their conceptual distinctions between life and death, among the human, animal, and vegetable worlds, are fragile and insecure. Heaven and earth are different to them in degree, not kind. The source of the problem is obvious: in such a static society, there is no room for a sense of an impersonal law flowing from a personal God. They pray, but scatter their petitions. I remember what you taught me, that my spiritual needs will be filled when the poor are not hungry, but if the poor here are not starving, what am I to do?"

Some days later the missionary wrote, "I have met an extraordinarily sensitive young boy named Phineas. I imagine he is what you must have been like when you were discovered on your island. He understands so well the deep nature of service. Phineas loves our Sunday meetings, not as much for the prayer and song as for the congregation of people and the chance to count heads. And this is what makes him so special: the boy does not keep his list of absentees for the purpose of chastisement, only to know who among the regular attendants is missing so that he might visit them, to see after their health, or to learn if there is something about our services that loses their attention. He cherishes his visits to the sick, and every day he walks through the church garden, swinging his machete to cut for them one of our delicious mangoes. Then he might talk to them a bit about my sermon, and I'm certain that he compensates for my shortcomings. He lives by example.

"Phineas knows that no one will come to God except by the coercion of his own soul. You and I have talked about the terrible mistakes made by the early divines. No branch of any church in the tropics is blameless. Your final sermon to my class at seminary has been my beacon. If it might have been better to leave the natives to their own multiple gods, and let them add to their pantheons with every new twist in history for which the old gods were unprepared, Jamaican Christianity is exhausted, and it is our duty as servants of Christ to repair the damage done in His name by the friars and devouts of earlier centuries, serving different crowns. I feel so often as though the crosses of Jamaica have become for the people as useless as any memory of a Congo river god. Look at the success of this ridiculous Rastafarianism. Marcus Garvey casts a metaphorical prophecy—that a king who will redeem the black diaspora shall be crowned in Africa—and when the slums of Kingston heard the news that Haile Selassie was the new emperor of Ethiopia, they mixed him into the gumbo of Caribbean slave religion and declared him the living God. Do you know that Haile Selassie once came to Jamaica? A hundred thousand Rastafarians (named for him, he was Ras Tafari,

Duke Tafari, before he was Haile Selassie) surrounded his airplane, and he hid inside for an hour. He had no idea what he meant to them. But I know what they mean to me, and I know my mission: to bring Christianity to the Christians, to find the cure within the poison."

After a cautiously encouraging reply from the bishop, the missionary wrote back, "You may remember that I mentioned Phineas in an earlier letter. This week has been difficult for him. His brother Aston (nineteen) comes to church every Sunday, but I don't know why. I suspect him of amusement. He is probably smarter than Phineas. I see him smile at his own thoughts, to which he doesn't give voice; he keeps himself entertained by the flow of his private observations."

The missionary wrote later, "Yesterday Phineas told me about an American woman who bought a small farm a short way from here. I suppose it is inevitable that the world's respect for the beauty of Jamaica would extend inland from the sea. Already the land near the water is too expensive for the locals. What will happen if the interior is colonized by the rich? The Jamaicans will be evicted from their own island, like Cherokee Indians!

"Her name is Yael. She visited me this morning, carrying two cameras. I predict she takes good pictures. She's an attractive woman, with a sort of familiar urban face, a certain type, clever and thin. She told me her story, or enough of it to explain what she is doing so far from the tourist colony. Her mother died a few months ago, leaving Yael too little money to support herself in New

York City without a job, but just enough to pay the rent and buy food if she lives in a poor country. She was tired of the life she had, and frankly admitted an affair with a married man, her third. Remembering Jamaica from a vacation six years ago, remembering the wistful tug of the countryside, the people, the possibility for discovery, she came here expressly to investigate a new way to live. She believes, as do I, that our world of surplus and luxury will soon be overwhelmed by the reproaching tides of history. Moving here, she says, gives her a head start on adapting herself to a new historical condition.

"She is interested in me, more interested than I am in her. She's not Christian, and she really doesn't need my ministry. Her hunger is emotional, and I have only so much time. She may imagine that I am grateful for the company of someone who makes sophisticated conversation, but the longer I'm here, the less I'm interested in urbane babble about ordinary unhappiness and ordinary cures. She said to me, 'I was unhappy.' I told her that the realization of unhappiness, as Thomas Merton said, is not salvation: that it may be the occasion of salvation, or it may be the door to a deeper pit in Hell. She greatly wanted to hear more about Merton, but I put her off. She wants to chat. I don't have time.

"And we have different missions. She came to Jamaica for art, she wants to make art and make of herself a work of art. She has in mind a photographic essay on her life in Jamaica. She says the church is beautiful and wants to take a picture of the garden. She promises that if any are sold or published, she'll make a contribution. I said that I would happily accept it now. She gave me fifty dollars, which I thought was fair. She wants to take a picture of *me,* but I said no. I said, 'You give me the impression that you're probably a good photographer, and if your work is published, I don't want to find myself immortalized as *Missionary in Jamaican Church.* She asked me, 'Is that your only reason?' I said, 'No. You may show more of me than I care to know about or have others know about.'"

Sometime later he wrote to the bishop. "Bad days. Aston (Phineas's brother) and Yael have discovered each other. She has been taking his picture, naked. She has him stand in waterfalls or on rock ledges. She poses him in profile before the sun and then the moon. He obliges. A pastor can't afford an easy moral shock at the varieties of human needs and pairings, but for her to prey on someone so young and so disposed towards sin makes me sick. A white woman who comes to the Jamaican hills for a lover is like the old slave traders casting an appraising eye on sturdy, dark flesh. I feel badly for Phineas."

The bishop did not respond. A few weeks later the missionary wrote to him again. "I should have known. Yael worships Gaia. Surely you've met Gaia the Goddess, Gaia the single organism we call Earth, Gaia the essence, Gaia the great female source of power, Gaia the Earth Mother, Gaia the land, Gaia fertility, Gaia fecundity, Gaia that part of the dual nature of divinity abandoned by men, not humanity but men, in favor of the sky god. Yael told this to me. She then asked if she could tape the singing at our Sunday service. I told her no. I said that the singing is sacred and there is no good reason for me to transform private ceremony into public performance. The next day she came around again and told me that the more she thought about it, the more she agreed that the incredible singing of the choir should never be recorded by someone who was not here to get closer to God. She said this with all sincerity, and then I sinned, I made a joke. When she said, 'closer to God,' I responded, too quickly, 'You mean closer to Goddess.'

"'What is that supposed to mean?' she asked.

"'It's just a silly joke.'

"'No, it's an insult.'

"'If you think so, then I'm sorry.'

"'No. I don't accept your apology. If I were to make silly little jokes about Jesus, would you let them pass?'

"'By training and prayer, I think I've learned to do just that. I hope I have.'

"'But it would hurt if I made a joke about Jesus.'

"'I'm not at a high enough spiritual level for it not to.'

"'So we're supposed to transcend our pain.'

"'I think so.'

"'To be big tough men, big cruel men for whom pain is not the primary message of distress but a personal challenge to overcome, to endure the agony.'

"'Like our Lord Jesus Christ.'

"'Instead of weeping like the Goddess, instead of weeping and wailing and trying to set things right, like Gaia. Motherfucker.'

"That's what she said, and you should hear it, too.

"'I'm sorry,' she said, 'that was wrong of me. I was behaving like a Christian. I should have expected this. You think I'm overreacting, don't you?'

"'I don't think so.'

"'Yes, you do. You think that a little joke about the Goddess is just that, a little joke.'

"'If it hurt your feelings, it wasn't funny.'

"'But if I'd laughed, and only later realized how much you hurt me, you might have prided yourself on your own wit and maybe even respected me because I could take it, because I could take your teasing, take it like a man instead of weeping like a woman, weeping at your feet like the Goddess, the inconsolable Goddess.'

"'I can see your point.'

"'I didn't make a point. Men make points, not women. Men make points because that's the world to them, spears and points and pricks, that's the world of men, a battleground. I didn't make a point. I just spoke from my heart. I let down my guard. I tried to be friendly with you. You're an educated man, you want to be a wise man, so I took you seriously. But your little joke makes me see my own mission in the hills more clearly. Yes, my own mission. We're competitors, aren't we? You represent the embassy of the sky god, the god of the tourists, the god of money. I have to try a different way of being. I have to let my life be like a whisper to them. I have to build a cathedral invisible from the air. You teach them that the body, the land, the woman, all of this is only in the way of the mission, all of this has to be redeemed. You teach them to burn the sacred trees. It's not that the land is profane, you're too modern for that, it's not that the poor are godless and heathen, you're too sensitive and guilty to keep reading that sermon over and over. The world knows that story and doesn't want to hear it anymore, so now you say that the poor have so much to teach us, but their wisdom has to be transubstantiated, it has to be changed, it can't be what it is, you won't permit anything to just be what it is. I'm glad you made your little joke, maybe it was Gaia speaking through you, warning me that you're the one who has to be tamed, you're here for the Father in Heaven, but that wild beast you serve so blindly is really the demon of all demons.'

"And then she left. I was a broken man. In my sermon that week, I could say nothing without hearing the long insipid warble of my voice. I took as a humiliating patronage the kindness of my parishioners. I couldn't tell anyone what was the matter with me, which forced an estrangement. And what did I give them? I looked at my congregants and saw them trapped with me, trapped by me. Yael knew she would offend the balance here by recording them singing because the tape would show that my flock uses the church not to be closer to God but only for the acoustics.

"They come to me because they have nothing left. Maybe this is the way faith begins, but I don't like it. I'm sick of the language of faith. We tell them: Yes, you have been degraded; Yes, in part by the religion I want to revive for you, because nothing remains of Paradise but your faith; Yes, faith alone won't feed your children, but without faith their bread will turn to ash. I know all of that. And I hate it. I hate the rhetoric of the religious party line, the stickiness of professional compassion, the tone of consolation ensorceled by greed. Greed for congregants and converts.

"I stopped talking. I wrote Phineas a note, telling him to tell the people that I was on the warpath against gossip. My silence, to avoid all that steams out of me, appeared to them as a sensational achievement. I wrote 'hello,' 'good-bye,' and 'thank you' on three white file cards. When a few small boys threw rocks at me so I would yell at them, I showed them 'thank you.' I kept this going for a week, and I felt much better."

It was two months before the missionary sent another letter.

"I am not naive. I know the ways that people deform themselves. If I didn't, I would have no claim on wanting to make the world better. And I admit that I probably know some aspects of the world only by rumor or refraction through magazines, television, and public scandal, but if I don't have the experience of sin, I can smell it. The world of sin clings like smoke. The fires are here in Jamaica.

"I heard the story from my laundress's husband, who heard it from someone else. I knew this much already: a few weeks ago Yael and Aston moved into a village some miles deep in the bush, where the people have no enemies and few gods. There's no television there, the only entertainment is community. That's why she wanted to go. One night, so I was told, everyone was stoned—on ganja from Bob Marley's personal plantation, where else?—and they built a bonfire. The people banged on drums of their own design and danced.

"According to the story, Yael commanded the center of the circle around the fire. She invited Aston to join her. You've seen the Jamaicans dance, you know how unrestrained they are, how sexual. Couples here dance close enough to be hanged in Arabia.

"Their dancing progressed beyond simulation. Yael, so I was told, made love to, or at least had sex with, Aston while everyone watched. And apparently, while she was having sex with him, she offered herself to one of the men nearby, and if what I heard is true, she took Aston and the other man together.

"Here's a surprise: that's not what bothers me. I'm telling you, I know about group sex, I know about the orgiastic current in the world. The horror of this episode is not what happens among some stoned fools wasted in the hills. Let them stay there. But the people in my town know the story and treat the event as just another episode made of the world's bundled energies. They don't particularly care. And Phineas! Phineas asked me, 'Sir, what is an orgy?'

"'An orgy. Yes. Well. Let me tell you that 'orgy' is a way of saying 'contradiction of God's desire.' Or the perversion of God's desire as a rampancy of desire. We speak of an orgy of violence, or an orgy of shopping.'

"But the boy knows what's going on by the bonfires. I fear he may already be lost, because even hearing about such hot, radioactive desire will itself begin a chain reaction of desire."

...

The bishop called. "Leave the woman alone. Draw a circle around the church and the people in the community whose faith you count on, and become the lighthouse for everyone else. Ignore Yael and her people. You've heard of witches? Yael is the real thing. This woman enchants her people with pleasure they cannot afford. The more you engage with her, the weaker you become. This is the formula for her success. We can't burn her, so ignore her. If witch burning would end witchcraft, I'd build the pyre myself, but it doesn't."

"What about her followers?"

"You have to ask yourself why people take such risks with their souls, and then ask yourself why some people protect themselves, why some people are faithful."

"Out of fear of God."

"Fear of God, yes, respect for terror, yes, but not love for Him. Discern who among your flock are faithful out of love. For the rest, they'll always be torn between opinions. Their faith will always be a battleground of resentment for bad luck and prayers not answered."

The missionary asked the bishop how he should proceed among the contradictions in his advice.

"I don't see contradictions."

"You'd kill her if you could."

"No, I'd kill her if her death would stop the plague."

"But if I ignore her and she continues . . ."

"She will."

"Then what do I do? I need a sign."

"She is the sign."

. . .

There was a long silence after this.

Tom heard a rat in the corner of his cell. "She is the sign? She is the sign of what?" It was the man in the next cell. The sounds of the prison were coming back. The man in the next cell called out, "Are you there?"

"Yes."

"What happens next?"

"I don't know." He had heard the story as he pronounced it, and nothing new was coming to him. "That may be the end."

"That's not how a story ends."

"I'm sorry. I don't remember anything else. It's not my story. It's the hanged man's story."

The light went on overhead, the naked bulb in a wire basket. The guard pushed a tray of food through the slot in the door: meat patties, a few bananas, coffee.

The guard looked in. "You don't know what happens next?"

"No."

"I think there's more." The guard went away for a few minutes and returned with another plate of food. "Eat this. You've been talking a long time."

"Thank you," said Tom.

"Everyone is listening," said the man in the next cell. "I pass it along as you tell it."

Tom finished his meal and lay back on the cot, floating in a mood of calm regret.

When he asked himself, "Why is this story part of my punishment?" he heard himself answer. . . .

...

The bishop's command to leave Yael alone sent the missionary into a week of dejection. He wandered through the village, inviting himself into the hovels of the poor and overstaying the tentative welcome offered him by the community. Because he returned their hospitality with so listless an effort at making them understand what he was doing in their houses and in their lives, the little goodwill he was earning for himself and his mission eroded with every meal he begged. When he understood this, he wrote another letter. "A terrible week. I became fogged with an obscure, interior confusion, and my happiness perverted by a sad, lost restlessness. My crisis was less about faith than my ability to honor my convictions. I am here to serve the poor. I reject the cheap piety that would have me say, 'I am here to learn from them.' I will earn redemption in the fight with a community's sin. You are wrong about my staying away from Yael. When Alaric, in his march on Rome, was told of the great army massed against him, he replied, 'The thicker the grass, the easier it is to mow.' I need Yael. I need an enemy. I need a battle."

...

Late that night, the missionary followed the beat of drums to Yael's camp. The moon was waning, and he brought his lamp and stayed off the trail. He pushed his way through ferns, through patches of wild pineapple. Countless fireflies blinked amid the pines in unison.

And then he was there, on the hill above Yael's camp, watching men and women he knew, some from church, on blankets surrounding the bonfire. The couplings were faster than he expected. Men and women met, fell into each other, were supported by others, and in turn supported them. People were quiet and, when finished, retreated to the edge of the circle. Yael put a blanket on a man's shoulders, brought beer to another. Then she entered the circle. Three men and a woman wrapped themselves around her, filling her body.

It was something like snakes, and something like archery, each of them pulling the other as a hunter pulls the bow, Yael alert to the pleasures of the others until it was her turn, when she coiled her arms tight around her lovers, and the missionary saw and was certain that Yael felt conscious of nothing else, faces, skin, wet fingers, the hair that brushed her breasts; her body seemed to vanish in widening circles that leaped farther and farther, beyond thought, and then her voice took flight like an arrow.

At Yael's release, eight arms rocked her. Rejecting their consolations, she twisted into misery, sobbing. Her friends held her tight. After a time, and how much time passed the missionary could not say, she hugged the men and the woman one at a time, speaking quietly to each, offering and accepting assurance.

The missionary stepped into the firelight.

"What did you see?" she asked. She opened herself to him. He looked.

"I saw you flung out of space."

"Did you see me cry?"

"Yes."

"Because I was embarrassed and ashamed of myself. As embarrassed as you would be."

"I doubt it."

"You think it's easy? Begging for release with the group brings up every embarrassing torment of compulsion and all the energy we use to deny that compulsion.

When the orgy ends, we hold each other with our two
bodies, the etheric and the physical, and this hug means
more than coming five times in one night; all of the frenzy
builds for nothing more profound than these delicate
hugs. In times of trouble, we have to affirm our trust; how
we do that is a matter of custom. Do you understand the
etheric hug?"

The missionary did not.

"The soul remembers what impresses itself on the
body," she said. "And the etheric body makes itself known
through conscience. But conscience cannot always be
trusted."

"Why not?" asked the missionary.

"What feels like conscience is not always so. Sometimes the fear of freedom speaks in the same voice. Fear
tells you that it's my fault you want me. That your wanting me is a sin. But let's take this apart. You want me,
but you're afraid of losing yourself in me. You could be
married and be afraid that if you want me and I give
myself to you, then you can't have your marriage, because
your wife won't be able to share you. But if the whole
community drops that drama of jealousy, and we all respect one another's compulsions, and overcome them
together, and spread love and trust, then we can tame
God's fearful voice. The Lumarians are training the fear
of God out of his little red shell."

The name stopped him. "The Lumarians?"

"That's what we call ourselves. The Lumarians. The
Light People. We have returned to the beginning of the

journey. Adam and Eve were Light People, automatons guided by Messengers of Light."

"The Messengers are separate from you? You're puppets?"

"Stop making fun of me. The intimidated fearful conscience, the image of God, turns to violence, and then the scarred etheric body drowns the physical body in blood."

"You're elevating sex to a level of worship."

"Oh, stop it. We're using sex as a ritual in the service of worship, not as the object of worship. You've seen how strong we are, how beautiful. They're different now, my people, you can see that, can't you?"

"You're not worried about disease?"

"We're clean."

"Then fine."

"You don't think it's fine."

"What can I do? What are we supposed to have, a soccer match between your side and mine?"

"They're the same side. I'm trying to bring them together. I want to heal the split between night and day, between waking and dreaming. I want to heal the world of hallucination, the projection of fearful desires. I want you to stop thinking of me as a succubus."

"Kind of hard not to."

"I see you're still flip. You know I find that offensive, but given that I've changed, I'll tell you the truth, it's kind of attractive on you. Your sarcasm is sexy. You should join us."

"You know I can't."

"I know you think you can't."

"I won't, then."

"You could if you wanted to. You should see what I'm doing. I've given them the power of the feminine. Jesus and the wound on his side, the labial wound, the wound made by the point of a spear, by a point, by one of those manly points. I want to bring them together. A return to androgyny. There's a universal religion inside all of us. Look at the people who are with me. You can see the power they have now. This is the power that starts a real revolution, because it starts from a necessity that's larger than the usual struggle for land and resources. Jamaica is the place for this revolution to begin. The people are so broken and so holy. Why did reggae become so popular around the world? Bob Marley was the kind of man who comes along every two thousand years! The Africans, at home and in their diaspora, are the great challenge to the world now. No other group is so low. No other group needs so much help, and the reason they are beaten down is that the first world knows what threat they carry within themselves that they don't even know they possess."

"Then good luck with your Lumarians."

"Your problem is obvious and pathetic. You want to experience the spiritual, but you can't let go of your ego. You won't face the power of your instinct."

"I know what's there. I control it."

"Then you'll never have illumination."

"Illumination is a luxury. I'm just here to feed some hungry children."

"And you want them to stay children. Let me show you what else we do."

...

The missionary returned to his church and wrote a letter to the bishop, describing some of what he'd seen.

"She brings all the members of her new community into a circle every morning. She asks them to share their dreams of the night before. When a dream is particularly strong, she asks everyone to make that dream into a play. She assigns them roles to perform the dream's allegory of desire, impulse, apprehension, sensation, and memory.

"She tells them, 'Now we will find out what our dreams really mean. Shared and acted out, our private dreams become our collective dream. If we share one another's deepest connections with open hearts, with love, the day will come when we all wake up together having dreamed one dream. We will know what to do. Each will take her part in the pageant without assignment. Each will make his mask or costume, and all of our words and music will come together as we dreamed them, without rehearsal, without script. And then we will spread our message across the island, and then around the world. And this will be like love.'"

...

The missionary read the letter and then sent it, knowing that the bishop would recognize madness. He reflected on his insanity, which was really nothing more than an inconsistency he refused to resist or hide.

Phineas was in the chapel when the missionary went to pray.

"I've bewitched myself, Phineas. This isn't Yael's fault. This is my fault. I'm in trouble. I feel like I'm cured now, but it's too late for what's about to happen to me. If I confess my errors when I go home, if I am rational and clear about all of my mistakes, if I tell them that jungle fever deranged me, I'll never get another church. I have ruined myself. I entered the ministry with fantasies of the same success that Yael dreams of, the kingdom of heaven on earth. I had spiritual fire, and I wanted to burn all the deadwood in the world. I had such contempt for the old men and their droll caution against religious excitement. Now I'm wise. Failure begets wisdom. Did you know that? But what do I do with my wisdom?"

"The bishop doesn't want you to see her anymore."

"You've been talking to him?"

"Every day."

"Is he coming here?"

"This is bigger than you."

The missionary wrote this letter to the bishop: "What are you telling the boy? Fine, I accept your pri-

vate connection with him. Phineas will come to the seminary, eventually, of course he will. I've been grooming
him, and you see what I see. He'll become important, I'm
certain of it, probably of greater meaning to our movement than you or I. I know your limits. I respect you and
I love you, but I know your limits. Just let me finish here.
Let me find a way to limit the damage. This is a labora-
tory. The methods we discover in Jamaica to thwart the
demons raised by this woman can be our ammunition
everywhere."

The bishop did not respond, and the missionary
knew that his silence meant that he was now observing
the situation through Phineas.

...

The more he thought about the poor Jamaicans and
ministered to them in the most basic ways—visit the sick,
read to a child, clothes for the family whose shack burned
down—the more he hated them.

His hatred of the Jamaicans spoke in the same tones
as his voice of conscience, as the still small voice he answered on his way to ordination, as the voice of his voca-
tion. Was God calling him to racism? Did God hate the
Jamaicans? Why else make them suffer?

The missionary started a letter to the bishop:
"They're cursed. I've been here for six months, and I know
this now. There's no other explanation. There's no reason to stay. They're cursed. They won't change. They

can't change. They shouldn't change. God cursed them, but I'm not on His side this time. I'm on their side."

He tore up the letter and burned it in his sink and washed away the ashes and then scoured the sink.

This is not the obvious story, he told himself. I am not just a repressed man of the cloth who can't control himself when a whore makes herself available. It can't be that simple. There has to be something more, I can't be the victim of such an old story.

But what else is there? he asked himself. There is no other story. It's the same old story, and if it is, and we know so much now about ourselves, then I should be able to control the story. I want to know both endings.

He started another letter: "Between Freud, Jung, and Lévi-Strauss, what's left? I believe in God in spite of the academy's evidence that faith is a social construct, that religion fills needs that are purely—what, social? The study of religion thinks itself clever for taking apart all of the pieces of religion, but the scholars miss the evidence that's in front of them, that religion is made of broken pieces because the infinite God could not express His infinity in the physical world without shattering. So God shattered, and the pieces were worshiped instead of God in His all-embracing singularity. I understand that, I understand that, I understand that. Fine and good. Fine and good."

He burned that letter as well, and buried the ashes.

But he wasn't going crazy, he also knew that. He was exhilarated by his stupidity.

He started another letter: "I have reached the limits of intelligence. I don't mean that I have solved the problems of physics, well, actually, perhaps I have, and all I lack is the math. But never mind that, I don't mean that. This is what I mean: there is a God. I know there is a God. And we cannot do what He asks of us, because we're an experiment that failed."

And then he burned that letter, mixed the ashes in water, and drank them.

He wrote another letter.

"I went into the chapel and prayed. I prayed for strength and guidance. I prayed for my parish not to be destroyed for the sake of my weakness. While I was there, in the church, on my knees, I heard the first drum of the evening from the Lumarian village.

"The breeze rose from the shore. Cars coming back up the mountain brought home the women who worked as maids for the hotels. I am surrounded by people who have never left the island. This is when I feel the age of the people here, their exhaustion, their resistance to change, their enslavement. Night falls, and the air carries the sound of a motorbike, and a guitar, and someone screaming, and I am in love with the matter of their helplessness, of my absolute inability to help them, and my sure knowledge that no one can help them. So I am in love with their ancient souls, and jealous of them for still owning a vitality that in my ancestral line was sapped probably by the end of the Middle Ages, when my forebears left the farm for town. I don't see anything here to save. I see people alive, in their lives, making whatever of their lives they can, and that their attention to me and attendance to my mission reflects only on the basic human goodness that calls for decent treatment to strangers. I reflect on this goodness and loathe the whole system that takes advantage of someone else's life and says of it that I know better than you what will give your life meaning.

"I stayed up last night, sitting on the porch, listening to the drums, waiting for them to come down the hill. I thought about sex. I thought, Perhaps she's right. There really is an aristocracy of sex, you see. When you cross the line into this Versailles of the mind and body, you enter the world of permission, and permission is privilege, and privilege bestows grace, and grace imposes itself as an oppressive force on everyone not directly touched. Like religion.

"Here they are.

"With steel drums and whistles, with tambourines and flutes, Yael and her cadre of sex warriors return to the town. I am drinking a bottle of Coca-Cola, which I opened, then poured out half the soda, and filled back to the top with rum.

"They greet old friends with the gracious calm of the wealthy returned after a summer in Tuscany. They have lost their quiet misery. I would say that there is nothing impoverished about them anymore, they have lost their beaten patience, the perception that time is stopped around them, that everything in their nature is old and exhausted; no consolation, no resuscitation possible.

"In their return to the town, I see such confidence. How can I make sense of this? It is all in the way their hands move in the air. Here, picture the daughter of a very rich man, the teenage daughter of your wealthiest supporter. You're in the living room of his mansion. You're there for dinner. The man is a bit of a monster, filled with his own importance, and his personality is impenetrable though charming. You visit her father because he has enough money to build a new wing for the seminary. He'll support you because he wants his daughter to meet you, to learn about God from you. He believes that you're a man whose presence might shine on his daughter's life. Now the rich man's daughter, all seventeen years of her, sits beside you on the arm of a beautiful couch. As you teach them a bit of Bible, the rich man is curious about God and has many opinions, all of them ordinary though sincere. And then his daughter asks you about God, she asks you about God and faith, especially your own faith, the story of your faith, your struggles with faith. She looks you in the eye. This rich girl's insult is that she appreciates you, she listens to your answers, she considers the implications of what you have to say, but her gracious smile, her strong posture, and the smooth skin on the inside of her wrists are all violent, disgusting assaults on you. She likes you! She tells you so, that she likes you! There's the insult, appreciation. And how are the Lumarians like the daughter of a rich girl? They have the same hands. How does the daughter of a rich man move her hands? At table she sits with one hand in her lap while she eats, unless she needs them both to cut something. The unused hand rests patiently on the napkin in her lap. When walking, her hands, like a Lumarian's, move freely in the air, sometimes reaching away from her in sheer delight of the flow of things, fingers spread to catch more of the air, even the smells of the air. When she goes to Paris, her hands catch the aroma of the bakery. I had never seen that gesture from a Jamaican before Yael came to the parish. Her followers were used to more activity, harder work. And this is what has changed in them, they have lost all their necessary, justified fear of the world. Lumarian hands move freely.

"My thoughts have turned angry instead of sullen, and I like them for that, instead of my self-inflated piety, always trying to feel the way I think I should feel. It is all so simple to me now; emotion, a moral life, what matters, what can slide.

"A small cloud passed over the town and rained on the parade. No one in Jamaica prepares for the daily rain, in destitution's rags, everyone is always ready for whatever the sky god offers. There's nothing to say about the mountain rain that isn't obvious, but Yael looked up at the clouds and called to them, 'Not today!' And everyone laughed and joined her, pointing to the sky and calling out, 'Not today!'

"They pound their tom-toms and chant their own songs and the sky clears. But this is no miracle, the sky

clears after every rain, the people here are not stupid, but
the villagers are—I don't want to say superstitious—I want
to say . . . I want to say that a people eager for entertainment will accept an event as a miracle if their commitment
to the idea increases the entertainment value of whatever
follows. Here's a thought for you, my teacher: faith offers
better drama—or comedy!—than skepticism. Skepticism
shatters the possibility of coherent meaning, leaving a col-
lection of pointless shards strung together only by
mathematical coincidence, and no valid mystically obscure
significance to induce revelation. So, for its own amusement, the town gives the credit for the sunshine to Yael.

"The Lumarians applaud her, and shyly she curtsies.
She offers her hands to the children, who join her in a
circle. She teaches them a song:

> O sun, O sun . . .
> O giver of life . . .
> O sun, O giver of life . . .
> We are all one . . .
> O sun . . .
> Spirit in the flesh,
> We are made of woven clay,
> In the hands of the sun,
> In the fingers of each ray,
> We find we are one,
> In the hands of the sun,
> In the fingers of each ray,
> We are all one.

"They have such beautiful songs here, and she gives them something so dreadful, and they take it; why? Everyone is singing along with her. Do you understand how awful that lyric is, how empty? There's a reggae song, 'Jah Penetrate to a Tenement Yard.' How can anyone exchange such powerful immanence for such weak transcendence?

"'Let us bring our gods together,' said Yael, leading the children across the road to the church, where I sit on the porch.

"She's singing one of our old hymns, 'And Did He Walk on England's Shores?,' but for England she substitutes Jamaica. The crowd takes it up. I have never heard it sung so beautifully before; the hymn that belongs to this church, reinvigorated with sex. There's no other word for the new element. Religion defiled and then made sacred again. I'm crying.

"Now she's telling everyone about a dream that she had last night, and a dream that Aston had."

...

"I had a dream last night," said Yael. "I dreamed that God was frightened, but in that dream my name for God, the image of God, was nothing more than my own intimidated conscience, and this frightened image of God wanted to kill. I saw God's carapace of fear behind God's blinding light, I saw God from a cleft in the rocks, and that cleft was but a crack in God's carapace of fear. God let me see God's creation through God's eyes, but God's red, dimmed tide of jealousy obscured the beauty God had made. I wanted to coax God, and patiently teach God, that the fear of universal love is God's enemy of life, and that the enemy of life is also the enemy of God, and that God could be the enemy of God's own creation if God remained in fear.

"And then, in my dream, God answered from inside God's cloud with a dream, because God was too frightened to speak directly. God could answer only with another story, since God's creation is just another story God told the empty universe, like a melody in the dark, for comfort. So God presented God's new story, and when I woke up, I told Aston the dream, and he stopped me as I began, and finished the story as I had dreamed it, because God had given Aston God's same dream. God wants us to show you God's new dream."

The Lumarians formed two circles behind Yael. "God dreamed that I dreamed that I was Bob Marley. God dreamed that I dreamed that I was Bob Marley when his mother was living in Delaware. God dreamed that I dreamed that I was Bob Marley and I was nineteen, and God dreamed that I dreamed that I went to Delaware to be with my beloved mother."

And one of the circles gathered around Yael.

"God dreamed that I dreamed that I worked in a factory."

Yael imitated the rigid movements of a young man trapped in repetitive motion, the slave of a machine, repeating a sequence of gestures, passing something along, tightening a bolt, returning to the first piece of the sequence.

One of the old Lumarian women stood before the second circle. "But why did Jah send Bob a ticket? Why, at that moment in his life, did God want Bob off from his native island of Jamaica?"

The second circle opened, and within it, two Lumarian boys held the poles on which they'd mounted an Ethiopian flag, ten feet long and six feet high. And on the flag they'd sewn the outline of an airplane, and on the plane the royal crest of Ras Tafari, the emperor Haile Selassie. Aston was behind the flag, wearing an army uniform and a stiff-brimmed officer's hat with gold braid.

The woman said, "Because when Bob left Jamaica to be with Bob's mother herself, who came to Jamaica but Ras Tafari?"

The circle around the flag broke into two lines, making a landing strip for the emperor's plane.

While the plane landed, Yael as Bob toiled on the assembly line, without feeling the vibration of what was happening in Kingston.

When the plane stopped, the two men raised the poles, and Aston stepped out into the Jamaican sun. The Lumarians knelt, crying, "Ras Tafari! Ras Tafari!"

Aston played the emperor's confusion and his fear. When the crowd moved towards the plane, he hid behind the flag. Now Aston started to sob, loudly, like a child.

And then, in the other circle, in Delaware, Bob Marley stopped working on the assembly line. Yael raised her head, not as though she heard the cry but felt it deep in the soul of the planet.

Ras Tafari cried, and Bob Marley answered him with a song, "Three Little Birds," everyone knew the song and hummed along with Yael until she took the reggae out of the song and brought in the lullaby. Yael, as the Psalmist of Trenchtown by the command in God's reverie, Yael, in song, told the timorous emperor not to worry about anything because everything was going to be all right, no strange sentiment to a song, but had the dread savior ever considered the simplicity of such an assurance? Selassie stopped crying. Now quiet, he searched across the sea, across the horizon, for the source of his tranquillity.

When he found the direction of the heavenly voice and his eyes met Yael's, it was her turn for silence, and her turn to kneel.

Rising on the power of the sweet singer's devotion, Aston assumed the full dignity of Ras Tafari, the emperor Haile Selassie, the living God, the redeemer of Babylon. The crowd of Rastas at his feet formed again the two ranks that became his airport, and the banner-as-plane took off for that part of the churchyard that was Delaware incarnate.

The circle around Bob formed the two parallel lines that matched the rows of the other group, and now the four rows joined into two and then squared, then bent the square into a circle as the banner gathered Yael and wrapped around her as she must have dreamed it, joining her, joining Bob Marley, God's salvation, with Ras Tafari, God's salvation, two high beings, two nodes of perfection, discerned by the poorest of the poor in the worst of Jamaica's shantytowns, all living prophets, forged from a poverty of everything but spirit.

The circle became two long lines again, now leading the plane with its joined holy cargo up the steps of the church towards the pulpit, and not just the players but everyone in the churchyard joined the lines.

When the couple wrapped in the Ethiopian flag passed the missionary on the steps, the ranks broke and the ragged crowd followed. The missionary, not moving, split the crowd like a memory splits attention, and like a bad memory, he was kicked and knocked off the steps to the ground.

He grabbed his notebook and, looking up, saw something he had to write down: "A van with tourists stops. Someone takes pictures. I know what they're thinking, it's a festive day, they're seeing natives follow a pageant into a rustic church, and they see a man on the church steps, writing in his notebook. What a colorful fellow.

"And here's Phineas with a machete. He's chasing the plane into that rustic church. The mob runs after him. The tourists are taking pictures of this. I can see inside the church, the couple on the floor, the boy with the machete. He's telling them to stop. They won't listen. He's just a boy. They're laughing at him. I'm going in."

Later, he wrote, just for himself, not in a letter, "The bishop had told me that if he thought burning the witches would make a difference, he'd light the match. It was easy for him to play with medieval fantasies, he was on the phone. As I tell him from time to time, I was on the ground. I did what I could, and I'd do it again. I can't say I love being back at the seminary, but I suspect that if I stay here and make myself indispensable, I might find a place in the church's High Command, and if not, I'll ask for a second chance on a mission, and if they're smart, they'll let me go. What happened in my parish would never happen to me again. Couldn't let a boy do my job. I've got experience now. The challenge will never go away. The next time I'll tell her to keep to the hills, and don't bring the party to town."

...

When the story was finished, Tom was taken to his cell, where his friends were waiting.

"So that's it," said Tom, bewildered by this encounter with the mystery of inspiration. "Do you think the hanged man was Aston? Or was he Phineas, telling the story with the ending he wanted?"

"That's not the story," said the old man. "That's not the end of it. There's more. That was for you. The missionary's story freed you from your dungeon, but nothing changes for us. That was not the story for which the hanged man died."

"How do you know?"

"Listen," said the old man. "The ordinary sounds of the prison have returned."

Tom opened himself to the world around him, the familiar frightening sounds of boredom and agony made of competing music, the screams of beatings, the tragic howls of the deranged, blasts of rage from guards, their occasional casual gunfire, the dramatic hustle of the soccer yard, and the infinitely shaded implications of belligerence and supplication that formed the context of most prison chatter. The rhythms of the place, silent while the story flowed from him, now broke into those interfering tempos. This signaled the prisoners' noisy submission to their ordinary sadness.

"But that's all I can remember," said Tom. He tried to remember something else, but his mind was gray. He thought of making something up but feared his own hanging for fraud.

The old man had an idea. "Tell us about your childhood. Tell us who your parents were. Tell us about your work. We'll find the story buried in your childhood."

"But my story is dull," said Tom. "I have no good story except for the murder. Everything else in my life is small, fragmented. I have nothing elemental. In my family, we were never hungry, we were never poor, we were never rich. I didn't join the army. I watched television, I went to the movies, I listened to music. I never made love to an heiress or a great beauty."

The translator expressed this to the old man. The old man responded to the translator, "You have seen the clown in the circus, he tells us the story of pride and ineptitude. It doesn't matter that you think you have no story worthy of the name, this is only your bad judgment. We believe in a God whose Word is not boring. If, as you say, you have nothing interesting to tell, then it shouldn't take too long to pull the hanged man's story from off your tongue. Come, let's hear your boring tale now."

Tom started: "I was born in 1960. My father wrote songs, but no one sang them. He had enough facility with music to . . ." Tom couldn't finish the sentence. He wanted to say something about his mother. "My mother was a travel agent, and then she sold houses. My father was disappointed in himself, but my mother loved him and encouraged him. Are the barbs of the hanged man's story caught somewhere in the tangles of my parents' life, as it comes to me?"

"Hatred for yourself will push the hanged man's tale further away," the old man said.

Why not let go and tell his story, with all its pockets of boredom and dull shame? These poor men possessed the gift to comprehend him better than all the world. What a help and strength it would be if he could give them freedom. He was one of them, he was a criminal. Our illegal pursuits insulate us from the common business of life, we share that sensation of moral cold that makes the spirit shiver. We are here to contemplate our crimes, regard them as sins, and make a fresh start. And, failing that hope, as we have, then the second purpose of all of this, of isolation, is also right. We are dangerous angry men. We are not ready to return. We will only disappoint and hurt the world.

"Tell us your story now," said one of the men.

It was so hard to talk about his father, a creative man thwarted by— by what? How would these poor men, whose fathers lifted heavy things for a living if they worked at all, follow the story of a musician who made enough money for a house in Los Angeles and a condominium in Aspen? Even these words as he thought to phrase them made him sick and embarrassed.

But he pressed on.

"My father was competent. He could not sell his songs, but he understood other people's melodies, and he adapted them to fit different singers."

Was this even a story? What he had just said was commentary, not chronicle.

"There used to be these variety shows on television, they were like high school talent shows, with a host who sang and did comedy sketches with a group of regulars and a guest star."

This made him almost retch.

"I can't do this," said Tom. "My life story makes me sick."

"You must," said one of the men.

He breathed again.

"My father surrounded himself with successful failures. They made money but hated themselves. Cynical
men who wrote comic songs. They wrote song parodies."
My father used to sing,

"Buffalo Bill and Wild Bill Hickok
Had a shootout on top of Boot Hill.
They were fighting for the love of
The dance hall Madam,
Her first name was Karnovsky but they called her Lil."

My father and his friends believed that parody had
to be the final word, and finding the weakness in a form,
they killed it and held the corpse worthless from the start.
After a few drinks they would sing,

"Ooh baby, are you my baby?
Ooh baby, are you my baby?
Ooh baby, am I your Dad or your Mom?
Because, ooh baby, either way something is wrong."

Tom sat up, still with his eyes closed, nauseated by
the abstraction of his childhood.
"A variety show had a star, it's like if Bob Marley
had a weekly television show and every week a different movie star and a different singer were on the show.
The movie star would do comedy sketches with Bob.
Bruce Lee would be a guest, and Bob would join him
in a parody of *Enter the Dragon*. Maybe Bruce Lee would

play someone who was afraid of fighting. Or Bob would play a reggae singer who was deadly with his hands, but as a joke. And then let's say that every week there was a different singer, and this week, Bruce Lee was the guest star and Julio Iglesias was the guest singer. And Julio didn't sing reggae, and Bob Marley didn't sing romantic Latin ballads. So my father would take a Julio Iglesias song and give it a reggae beat, and he'd take a Bob Marley song and smooth the beat, give it a steady four-four beat, and add the violins. And then the two would sing in each other's styles. So that's what my father did for a living, except with Sebastian Cabot instead of Bruce Lee and Andy Williams instead of Julio Iglesias."

Tom tried to describe Sebastian Cabot to a prison filled with Jamaican murderers, tried to make them understand Sebastian Cabot, an always bemused professional Englishman who played butlers and foppish rich men on American situation comedies, but it was impossible.

Where was the hanged man's story in all of this? This wasn't a story, not really. What was a story? What was a specific story he could tell from his vague childhood? There were so few. Everything else was television.

"One of my father's friends was a joke writer. He wrote a newspaper column with the three best jokes he heard every other day. He sailed a small boat in the Santa Monica Bay, and my father envied him, so he bought a sailboat. The first day we went sailing, my father almost drove the boat into a seawall. We were going slowly enough to stop the boat just before disaster, but my father ran away from the front of the boat, I forget what he said, but he was frightened, and I could see that he was ready to quit. My father's fear was something I shouldn't have seen. I don't know how we took the boat back to the slip, maybe I turned on the engine, maybe he did, maybe someone gave us a hand. We went out again, and we learned to sail, but we never went anywhere. Out for a few hours and back, out for an afternoon and back. We never went anywhere. There's an island off the coast of Los Angeles, and we never sailed there. We should have gone, but my father was scared. And this changed my life, not having sailed to Catalina."

But this was a complaint. Maybe that's a form by itself, he thought, like a waltz or a tango. No, they wanted a story.

Nothing emerged from him that he could have remembered only because a hanged man needed a confessor.

"I was at a McDonald's once, and I picked at the french fries of the man sitting next to me. He yelled at me and made me buy him a new bag. Before the man was taken to be hanged, he said this to me: "The Caesar held the golden staff of the tribe of Judah. Shaped like a shepherd's crook, the staff curved at the top to end as a lion's head. The ancient craftsman had wrapped the staff in the folds of a symbolic fabric. With the staff in his hand, Caesar could easily ken the praetor's curiosity. Caesar explained the sacred relic.

"'There were once twelve brothers. They were jealous of the youngest and threw him into a pit. He was sold to slave traders and taken to Egypt. In later years, his brothers joined him. When their father died, Judah, the oldest, was compared to a lion. A lion guarding sheep. Now that's a puzzle, isn't it, Praetor?'

"'I am a soldier, my lord, who grew up in Rome. I'm not an expert on animals.'

"'But even soldiers think.'

"'Not on duty, my lord.'

"'You have no opinion?'

"'I want to know what Caesar is thinking.'

"'The lion who guards sheep seems at first to be the great reconciliation, Praetor. The predator shall guard the prey? The wild shall protect the domesticated? So the lion and the sheep both have to master their own natures. It's obvious what the lion is called upon to control, his appetite and power, but the sheep who allow themselves to be guarded by the lion must also fight their nature, their compulsion to panic and stampede. But there is an ancient prophecy, that the lion shall lie down with the lamb. So the lion will guard the sheep against other predators. Now, here's the riddle: the prophecy doesn't say what the lion will eat. If the lion has forsaken mutton, then he has to find other flesh. The lion cannot live on clover. But if he leaves the flock to hunt, who will stand guard? The lion shall guard the sheep, yes, but from whom and for what purpose? Listen to me, Praetor. The sheep make a covenant with the lion and stand as guarantors of the lion's reformed character. But this is a strategy. The cattle and the deer, seeing the lion and the lamb so close, observing the lamb's trust in the lion, approach the lion for protection, and he eats them.'"

Tom heard only the end of the story as it left him. All the detail that had filled him up, so full that there was no room left for Tom, all that detail was gone, and now Tom felt himself become complete to himself. He listened for the sounds of the prison and discovered only silence. Even the guards walked softly.

Tom's head fell to his chest. The men helped him to his bed and covered him with a blanket.

The prisoners considered the story left to them by the hanged man. The story passed quickly through the prison. No one understood it precisely, and its indeterminate meaning was solved only by collective agreement and even dispute. Societies for interpretation gathered in the cells at night, and in the yard during the day, the prisoners separated themselves into academies of two or three. They passed along to other groups their sense of the story as best as they could, and then the groups broke up and re-formed with the men from other groups. Each prisoner then made for himself a new friend with whom he shared the task and pleasure of unpacking the story, passing their vision of its meaning back to another prisoner, who in his turn had also made for himself a friend, so each prisoner became student of one and teacher of another, and the two of them together took the pieces of their own meaning and the meaning gathered from their students, passing that collation into the circulating rivers of meaning, where others in turn joined new students and new teachers and, after working the story through their own lives, brought those fresh renditions to someone older or wiser or simply someone new. No leader emerged or could emerge to pronounce the final commentary; the chain linked to itself in so many places that the entire prison quickly forged a steel girdle of teachers and students, all deciphering the enigma of what the hanged man told the American. The story tugged each man in a special way. It was not a simple story, but it was made of simple pieces. Each man heard the story in the voice of his mother or the voice of his father. Each man, to make sense of things, had to tear himself away from the story in favor of the reality of his own life. To understand the story, each, in the sessions of long study with his friends, first had to confess his crimes and sins.

Of the many informers among them, the power of the story of Judah's staff overwhelmed their routine impulse to run to the guards to barter every scrap of useful information for privilege, however small the bonus.

Life in the prison changed. No one fought. The yard was quiet, not silent, but to the warden, who heard the vibrant babble of the men at shared study one day about three weeks after the disclosure of Tom's hidden story, this culture of politeness was a frightening and inexplicable threat. He had searched for the right word and found "politeness" and said so to his wife.

"These men are the worst of the worst," he said to her, "and now they're as calm and agreeable as girls born to wealth and raised by loving parents."

The warden and his wife negotiated his career together, and she visited the prison the next morning. She opened his window and put her ear to the main yard and listened seriously for three or four minutes. When she brought her head back into the room, she told her husband to immediately call the minister of justice and security, and to tell him that an informer had given him the guarantee that a riot or an escape attempt was a matter of days away. She cautioned the warden to tell the prime minister that the informer, on return to his cell, was murdered.

The army responded to the prime minister's call after the minister of justice and security deferred to the prime minister. The minister of justice and security understood the risks in quelling a rebellion in an island prison when the culture of the island was little different, in so many respects, from life inside the walls. He assured the prime minister that half a dozen informers had been murdered before they had even informed, that the riot leaders were taking no chances and were getting revenge in anticipation of betrayal. So the prime minister gave his assent to the mission, and the prison's guards made room for soldiers who filled the prison one morning two hours before dawn. They tore about the cells, forcing the men to stand naked in the sun while dogs and experts in concealment searched through the prison for signs of the mass escape of whose imminence there was no doubt.

The prisoners obliged calmly. The soldiers chose a few of them at random, including the old man, to beat in front of the rest, and those who were beaten gave no resistance, so that the soldiers felt shame and reluctance for their cruelty.

By the time the men were hauled into the prison yard, stripped of their clothes, and locked in place naked, member to buttocks in a coiled serpentine, each had achieved a sanctified humiliation that accepted and contained his degradation. So completely and placidly and with such incomprehensible grace did the men receive this debasement that to the eyes of the soldiers, the men were clothed.

Of course no guns were found. The few knives that turned up, which the colonel in charge showed the warden, were of no consequence and in no way suggested the arsenal necessary for this many men to overwhelm armed guards and steel and stone.

Each of the men in line, without sharing a spoken word with his neighbors, knew in his heart that this spectacle, this theater of authority and power, could at any moment's alarm become, after one bloody hour, a mountain of corpses, but they did not and would not provoke an attack. So in peace they fulfilled the purpose of the hanged man's wretched need to unburden himself of the story held too long without an audience. The soldiers returned to the barracks. The warden's wife went home. The warden cleared his desk. The naked men in the yard were given their clothes, their papers, their wallets, their watches and rings, the chains and charms they had surrendered on entry, and told they were free.

Later, each would tell someone he loved, "You have a choice. There is destiny, yes, there it is, here it is, the unpolluted moment, the intersection of open possibility. And what do you do when you come to that moment? You meet the moment and then what? Fulfill, sacrifice, nullify, or evade?"

Tom walked out of the prison, his hair white, his nose broken. He stopped at the waterfront, a mile away. Across the harbor, cargo ships docked beneath cranes that loaded and unloaded with so little noise and so much activity that it seemed a conspiracy against the island. Someone is making money somewhere, Tom thought. I cannot save them all. He looked down at the water drifting slowly along the seawall, at the small fish feeding on the scum and the grasses, and as his vision expanded, as his eyes relaxed, the crabs hidden in the rocks caught his attention with their movement.

He was thinking about himself, not to think of his own self-disinterest, but to call this condition egoless would assign to him a stale, impossible transcendence. Tom lodged himself in the elements of the harbor, there he was in the sun, the rusting iron, seagulls, crab shells, the vendor selling mango ices from a wagon, Japanese cargo ships, a beer truck, the man and woman fighting over love, she chasing him, her tired rubber sandals slapping her feet, trucks and motorcycles grinding their gears, the air.

If on the quay his mother, in Jamaica and mysteriously still alive and walking on the same path, had seen him from a long way off, his form, his outline, his silhouette, what a mother knows of her son, and had she been wearing a watch, and had he asked her for the time, testing the disguise imposed by his destiny, yes, she would have heard something in this damaged stranger's voice that reminded her of the son lost to prison, and yes, with a freshly surfaced agony she would have given him the time, quick as panic that becomes riot, and then moved on.

Five

Horrible things happen. We all know this. A man kills another man. This happens every day. Now we know a few pieces of the story of one man who killed another man, in full mind of his actions. The murderer disappears from the world that knew him. He returns to the world under a new astrological sign, the ellipsis, the invisible constellations discovered by their effect, not their light. He has been missing from the world, but the world goes on, syntactically correct. Well, perhaps not correct or even legitimate, but full of its own sustaining sense.

To those who knew him, his life becomes a November field, all stubble after the harvest, cleared for the search for meaning. How did this happen? they ask one another. What did we really know about him? That question is the effect of his ellipsis. . . .

Now his return to a world without walls begins at a road under two signs, one marked RELEASE and the other LIBERTY.

Tom Levy, released into the world but not yet free, stood on the quay in the Kingston Harbor, thinking of his daughters, Perri and Alma. He was not so blank of past feelings; that the revelation in the Spanish Town Prison, so recent and yet already obscure, had wiped out all the residues of the murderous impulse he would never again call blind. This would have surprised him, but his emotions seemed to appear within him first as on a screen, and then, with his new freedom, he made a free choice to accept or deny that emotion's claim on him. So he saw the possibility of surprise for what had not changed within him, and left it alone.

The thought of his daughters brought him sadness. Perri was seventeen now, and Alma twelve. He made a choice to feel that sadness, and the more he considered the damage to their hearts, the more his pain rose in desire of taking back the hurt. No word from the family had passed his way since the day he signed the papers for divorce, or if it had, the news never penetrated his long trance.

He was impatient, he was hungry, he was lonely. The prison's revelations were not bread, and this was another revelation. "I am hungry. I am still Tom Levy," he said to himself out loud. "I am myself, and I have to leave Jamaica. Whatever purpose I served here, my own purpose or God's, this piece of my life needs to end. I am sorry for the hurt my daughters suffer, sorry for the horror I caused the family of the man I killed, and sorry that his place in the world is gone, but there is nothing I can do on this harbor's walkway to make the past different. I am here, and I want to be somewhere else. I don't know where I want to go. I don't know how to get there. I suppose this is a prayer."

He sat on the quay, waiting for the next thing to happen. Night came. He did not sleep. Morning came, and with it, pulling a child's red wagon, a brittle-haired blonde of something like fifty, though she could have been ten years younger and twenty years at sea. Her face was cracked from sun and salt, and her eyes bulged with delight, as though her skull could not contain the surplus of her joy. On the wagon was a large sail bag that she kept steady with one hand, but the going was awkward for her.

"American?" asked Jan Dodge.

Tom said, "How did you guess?"

"It's what I say to everybody. Breaks the ice. Can you give me a hand?"

Tom said yes again and let her pull the wagon while he walked behind her, holding the bag in place. It was a simple job, and Tom liked how even this little effort to help someone improved his day.

"It's the new spinnaker. The last one tore between Cancún and here. That was a leg. Do you sail?"

"Not really."

"Eddie and I are making for the South Pacific, but the long way, around Africa through the Indian Ocean, north of Australia. We started in Long Beach, California, and we had a fellow with us all the way from Mazatlán to Panama, but he got tired of us. I don't blame him. I'm telling you that because if you want to crew with us, you have to put up with us. No boat is big enough for people who don't get along. You look like a man who's ready to leave. You look like one of us, a little dangerous but not evil. Am I right?"

"I don't know how to answer that question."

"Everyone is marked. You spend enough time at sea, and when you pull into port, you have perspective. How many billion in the world today?"

"Six."

"The numbers don't tell the story. They don't lie, but they don't tell the whole story, which you get when you've been at sea long enough. Say there's six billion people. That's an impressive number. But that's only counting bodies. What do you know of the ancient Hebrew doctrine of the prime soul? That's the types, the types that are deeper connected than the fabrications of race and tribe. I want to introduce you to Eddie. I say there's not too many thousands of different prime souls, maybe six hundred thousand. Take New York. You walk in a crowd, you see faces, you see body types, and you see the mood in someone's eyes, the way that person looks at the world, whether he thinks it's all kind of funny, even the worst of it, or he's just beaten down by the world and doesn't have the peace to hold the world in any kind of detached appraisal. How many distinct types in New York? I don't mean commuter cabby doorman bartender model, I mean finer distinctions within and among them.

Crudely, I'd call your attention to the difference between the bald and the hairy, that the hairy mathematician and the balding athlete are types. Y. A. Tittle, being the founding idea of the bald jock, and any number of hairy Jewish boys at Columbia University are witness to the obvious connection between adolescent Jewish hirsutism and a stirring facility with figures. But I am also thinking about a quality that includes morphological categories yet goes beyond them. You have a feeling of familiarity with people in the world, and what does that come from? You know something about someone, a finer knowledge than a physical imprint gives you, it's the source of the impression. Am I making sense? Because if I'm not, stop me."

Tom said, because he knew she wanted this from him, "I don't quite follow."

"Take yourself, your special case. You're a man prematurely white-haired, a man obviously with some life under his belt." She held the moment, she was waiting for Tom to permit more of the lecture with a quiet agreement, which he gave.

She went on, "But I've seen this before, looking at a man's face and discerning a laminate of moral collapse, recovery, and collapse again. Now, that's one composite layer of what I see, but I don't see that on your surface, your surface skin has a shine, and I recognize this as a kind of shellac, it's a glaze, if you will, composed of two basic elements, one, your rueful contemplation of the tentative achievement of a new sobriety, and two, your hesitant fear that the sobriety is temporary. I see this here," she said, rubbing her thumb rudely and hard under his eyes, "in the reflective capacity of the bags under your eyes, your sad eyes. Shiny skin, wrinkles, a good sign of an old shame. But I'm talking to you because I know by your white hair, old man, that you're probably, which is enough for me, safe."

"A lot of men get gray hair when they're still young."

"Yours is white, not gray. And you have your eyes, those kind of eyes, my old friend, can't fool me. The reason you turned prematurely white is that your soul recoiled at the things of this world that your body had dragged it to witness. The soul does not participate! That's how people die before they die, the soul picks up and looks for daylight under the walls of the tent. The soul is God's ambassador to the will! The soul is more like a classical analyst than any kind of rabbi or spiritual teacher, you know, because the soul can only advise and watch, the patient has free will. Oh, the soul speaks, but the body rarely listens. This is a bit mixed up, I'm sure, but the thread is right, and if you crew with us, we'll work out the tangles. This is what I need other people for. I can't do this alone, or even with Eddie. The universe doesn't rest on my opinion of it, and this is just a provable theory only as I search the world for cases and find, when I talk about this, a harmonizing pitch in the spirit of whoever is listening to me. There's no growth without a good conversation. And my ideas, I have to confess, are a fever of the brain with me, because my humanity is marred forever by my constant searching of faces for analogues in my inventory. Faces and cases, of course, the thing within that comes through the beacon of the eyes and heart. But I've said too much already, and there's my man. Eddie!" she called her husband's name.

He waved back at her. He was on a wooden pier, beside a rubber dinghy with an outboard motor. Beyond him in the harbor, a few dozen sailboats were tied to orange buoys. Jan said, "This is Tom. He's thinking about shipping out with us."

"Let's start with lunch," said Eddie.

"Thanks," said Tom, for the rhythm of things. In what prime-soul category did Jan Dodge file her husband? He looked like a golf pro who'd been sacked for embezzlement, the boyish fifty-year-old with just enough smarts to know he was dull and dumb and incapable of success on the level of his rich golf students at the country club. This blend of self-knowledge and stupidity attracted people to him, gave his greed permission to run, but dangerous resentments propelled him towards disgrace. Now Tom could think only in types. Eddie Dodge was a chunky man disdainful of exercise but always active, cheerful in the wind of disappointment, with the wife swapper's glint in his eye, saying, "I know the route to contentment while pursuing malicious pleasure." But was he any of these, Tom wondered. Or did the theory of the prime souls allow that all suspicion is founded in the truth?

Tom couldn't help but ask, "Does each of us, in our bodies, contain one prime soul, a copy of the original prime soul?"

"Prime souls?" asked Eddie, winking at Tom as if to say, Did she bend your ear on the way? Well then, welcome to my life, but it's not a bad one, and I love her, so don't look to me for support against her philosophical attack. It was that kind of wink.

"No," said Jan. "The original six hundred thousand prime souls have been chopped and blended and spread throughout the world, so that the shards of each type of soul search the world to complete themselves. This is about community and friendship, the fellowship of cosmic similarities that speaks to us across the gulfs of loneliness. Like you and me right now. You can never feel complete the way the Platonic system promises because there's no perfect matchup of the other half of the torn dollar bill, there are millions of pieces among millions of people. Six hundred thousand is a big number, line up everybody in New York City according to your distinctions, and do you really imagine that you'd create more than a thousand rows? There's some souls that seem to predominate and others that are rare, the distribution isn't equal. But this is getting too ornate for you, and we need help loading the spinnaker into the dinghy."

Tom lifted the sail bag over his shoulder while Jan and Eddie brought the red wagon into the rubber boat.

She was right; as theologies go, Jan's was awfully gaudy, but at least it explained to Tom how Eddie Dodge could be the corrupt golf pro and so much else besides, how he could give the aura of corruption even if he had never so much as kept a library book past its due date.

Tom stepped from the dock into the boat. When his second foot left the dock, he realized deeply, profoundly, and ardently the distance he'd come, not in a measure of geography but of time and spirit, that he was now leaving the island of Jamaica, that he was off around the world with interesting lunatics, that he was going someplace new, someplace different.

Eddie took control of the outboard, and Tom unwrapped the dinghy's lines from the iron cleat on the dock. A thousand soul types in New York City? Tom let the thought drop as far as he could, and forced his way into the moment by watching Eddie Dodge steer the dinghy through the yachts. Tom read the names of the boats on their sterns, and where they came from. Here was *Jo-Ann* from Boston, *My Three Sons* from Boca Raton, *Sea You* from Galveston, *Jack Iron* from Newport, R.I. It seemed a snug world. Over the time that Tom spent with Jan and Eddie, he could never get used to the dull eccentricity of so many world cruisers, how to reconcile people so often boring with the high specific skills and courage they needed to steer small boats through storms a thousand miles from rescue. "Here she is," said Jan, as they pulled alongside a catamaran. Painted on both hulls was the boat's name, *Mimesis.* "Forty-eight feet long," said

Eddie. "Would you be nervous about sailing a cat around the Cape of Good Hope?"

"I don't know enough to answer the question. Have you done it?"

"Not yet, nor Cape Horn, either. We're scared but not afraid. You?"

"I don't know enough."

"We don't like to hurry. We can make the long passage from Cape Town to Australia in one leg, but the seas out there can be pretty high. Do you have an opinion?"

"It's your boat."

"But if we were to be hurt, if you were sailing this boat not quite single-handed but without our full ability to lead, could you handle things?"

"Why don't we sail for Cape Town and see what kind of sailor I am? If you don't want me after that, I'll get off."

"That's an answer," said Jan.

...

Great waves that followed others scared Tom when he met his first storm, but Jan and Eddie taught him how to surf the faces of the waves and, when the storm proved too ferocious, how to drag a parachute in the water to slow the boat and let the broad slick settle the following sea.

So the worst of his fear left him, and in the literal wake of that departure, Tom found room for new thoughts. He sat in the hammock between the hulls, eyes on the mast tracing arcs across the sky, until everything dissolved in motion. He was lonely with these strangers but wanted no comfort from them, and enjoyed them as he once should have enjoyed his children's friends. He had never cared for other people's children, the burden of his own took enough of his patience and spirit, but if he had them again, he would ask his children's friends, "What's the name of your favorite doll, who is your teacher this year, do you have an enemy at school?" He would take them to parks and let them stay as long as they wanted, and he wouldn't bring a book, he would watch them the way he watched the sky, and love them no less than his own.

He was in the hammock when Jan Dodge slapped his face.

"Get up!"

Tom covered his face with his hands as she emptied a large sack of garbage on him.

"We just crossed the equator, and you've never crossed before. And everyone who crosses the equator for the first time is a pollywog. Do you want to stay a pollywog?"

"Is this a joke?" Tom asked, spitting out eggshell and coffee grinds. He tasted something even uglier.

"Do you want to stay a pollywog?" asked Jan. "Answer me. Yes or no? Do you want to be a shellback?"

"Where's Eddie?" Tom worried that they were going to drop him into the ocean. So my punishment has finally come, he thought, the hanged man did not save me.

"There is no Eddie on this boat. There's only King Neptune and his bride. And I'm not the bride today, my little pollywog. Come here."

Jan twisted Tom's right ear and forced him to the stern, where Eddie sat on the end of the hull naked, his belly covered in grease from the diesel's oil pan. He wore a gold-foil party crown.

Jan picked up the boat hook and knocked Tom's shoulders with the handle. "Kneel in front of the royal baby."

Tom crouched down, facing Eddie's filthy stomach.

"He's not dressed right," said King Neptune. "He can't marry me if he's not dressed right."

Jan went below and came back with a yellow bra stretched between her hands like a cat's cradle. "Take off your shirt and put this on," she demanded.

Tom obliged her, seeing no choice.

"Come on," said Eddie, "join us. Kiss me. Kiss my belly." He said this in his own soft voice, putting aside King Neptune's bluster.

Tom reflected that his life had carried him to strange places, and now he was on the equator, closer to the sun that he had ever been, with the world of water around him. What did he have to lose?

He pressed his face into Eddie's gut, covering himself with slime, when Jan whacked his shoulders. His body folded around the pain, and he fell to the deck. Jan hit him again. "Stay down," she said, while Eddie pulled the storm sail out of its bag and spread more garbage on it. Then they wrapped him like a cigar and made him crawl out of it. Of course this is birth, he thought. I know that much.

And then they threw him into the ocean.

When he came to the surface, caught in a trough between waves, the catamaran was gone.

Tom treaded water, stirring the current and summoning the coldest layer six miles deep. A swell lifted him high enough to see the mast of the *Mimesis* coming towards him. He grabbed the hammock's netting from below, and the boat dragged him through the water. Jan and Eddie watched without comment as Tom swung himself to the hammock's leading edge, resting until he found the energy to pull himself to safety.

When he came back on board, Eddie was clean. Jan gave Tom a little printed card of a sea turtle.

"I don't know what it means," said Jan. "It's an old sea tradition."

Tom knew but kept it to himself. The sea turtle, like Tom in prison before release, is self-condemned to lasting sorrow and penal hopelessness, never mind that he owns the ocean.

They never spoke of this again.

So they sailed without crisis for a year, from South Africa to the Indian Ocean. They stopped in lonely Chagos and traded stories with the cruisers who cast off from shore and spend the rest of their lives at sea; they sailed below Sri Lanka to Malaysia, where a freighter cut across their bow with ten feet clear because the freighter had a bad spirit aboard and offered the ghost another ship to haunt, but Eddie wasn't afraid, "because I don't believe in Malay ghosts." Eddie taught Tom how to fix a diesel engine, and when they pulled into a harbor and needed cash, they'd find other cruisers with trouble and fewer skills and help them.

...

So a year and a half passed. By and by they stopped in Fiji, where the *Mimesis* dropped anchor in a lagoon on the coast of Taveuni Island, below a colony of bungalows on a low bluff.

Eddie said, "Look at this place. There's two well-fitted dive boats, and a few skiffs for fishing, but no sailboats. We could spend a few months here running sunset cruises and make some money, enough for a year."

"If they'll have us," said Jan.

"There's only one way to find out. Tom, you stay on the boat while Jan and I make a useful friend or two."

An hour later, they returned with Pete and Beryl Poole. From Pete's first "G'day mate," Tom pegged them for professional Aussies, an exhausting type, forever playing the role of the free man, but he wanted to pave over his wariness with some benevolence; they were innkeepers with years of forced affability, and perhaps after time they'd show Tom some of their despair.

The Pooles were in their forties, and there was something grim about each, thought Tom; he saw, underneath the manic friendliness, a defeated expectation. This would have made them sympathetic, but his caution increased the more he watched them. Pete was handsome and Beryl was pretty, without either being interesting to look at, like career officers stuck in the middle ranks, Tom thought. Their movements were precise and quick. Things happen slowly for a long time, and then everything is new and fast. Who are these people? Why are they here? Something begins with them. What?

"How long have you been here?" asked Tom.

"Okay, the story, quick," said Pete. "We're from Australia, we came here seventeen years ago and built the club from scratch."

Beryl explained, "The Taveuni Reef Club."

"Yeah," said Pete, drawling the word. "It's a club with no membership dues, but a club all the same. You don't come here unless you know what you're doing. We take expert divers only, there's no instruction, and the best come from around the world. The reef out there has coral fans—"

"That are six feet tall," said Beryl.

"And when you're down below, you can look up sometimes and see the bellies of a thousand tuna going down the channel. We're like you people, we gave up the rat race, as they call it, and followed our dream, to make money at what we did for fun, and what we did for fun was scuba dive. We have a boy, Alan, he's sixteen, and I expect you'll meet him soon enough. He's the boy I wanted to be, and I'm the father I wanted to have." Pete finished this self-congratulation with an astonishing giggle, a tee-hee-hee, just that. This repulsive trill convinced Tom that Pete's story, in its general outline, was true, but about the father's pride in his beautiful son, he knew that Pete was lying.

The couple poked about the boat, declared her "clean enough for the job," and so the business was set; Pete and Beryl would let them stay here on the island "until we all get sick of each other or until the business fails," and the *Mimesis* would take resort guests, up to six of them, for late afternoon-sunset cruises. The Pooles would split the receipts fifty-fifty, and feed the *Mimesis* crew four nights a week, drinks half price.

...

That night, Jan told Tom, "I don't trust them."

"Does Eddie?" asked Tom.

"Not really. Neither do you."

"No. What prime souls are they?"

"He's a chopped salad of chastised priest and vengeful disinherited firstborn, with some hunter thrown in for the fat."

"And Mrs. Poole?"

"Beryl is the neglected younger sister of a pasha's second-favorite concubine."

"You're making that up."

"I don't know what she is. She's strange. How about that for a category? Strange?"

"That fits all of us."

"And that's why we're friends."

"But we don't like her, and if she's strange and she's one of us, then we don't like ourselves."

"That's what makes us *strange*." Jan set an emphasis on the word.

Tom thought about Jan's appraisal, and the way that both of the Pooles incited images of displacement, first-born, second-favorite. What did Jan know about them? What did she know about Tom? Why were the Pooles in Fiji? Their reasons could be no less complicated than Tom's, the past sin, need to escape, nowhere to go. The self is everywhere.

The resort's guests, spending hours underwater, eagerly gave themselves over to the crew of the catamaran. In the late afternoon, a wind came down the channel, and the boat reached its noisy hull speed. With so little draft, Eddie raced above the coral heads.

Jan, wanting to know more about Alan, invited him to sail. He was quiet on the boat, but he jumped to every task. She told Tom, "I don't get him. I don't understand him. But you, Tom, have been studying that boy. You're not ready to say, though, what you suspect."

She was right. Tom had watched Alan, but nothing yet added up. The boy kept to himself and seemed to have few friends. Tom saw him early most mornings, when he paddled a blue kayak through the lagoon carring a spear gun. He always returned with fish. And during the day, Alan was always moving, always doing something, hauling gear to the dive boat, carrying furniture in or out of bungalows, varnishing the teak in the main lodge. There were a dozen other white children like Alan on the island, most of them the children of innkeepers, but whatever their society, Alan either wanted no part of them or they, sensing his difference, kept him out of their games and conspiracies. He seemed perpetually on a quest, as though every moment were the crucial test of an initiation ritual. The boy didn't seem to mind his isolation from the gang; or rather, whatever burdened him filled his inner life with more than enough noise to cover the buzz of rejection. Besides, the other children went to school, while Pete and Beryl followed a course of home tutoring. When Tom asked why, Beryl answered, "Are you an expert on education? Are you a father?"

Tom answered, "No." This was no time to tell her his story, how he had been a father of beautiful children and, by his own agency, had thrown them away.

"Then you don't know. You don't know what schools are like, do you? You don't know what they teach."

"It's been awhile since I was in school."

"Right. It has been. We're teaching Alan all he needs to know. And don't interfere. It's our way."

...

After four weeks, with fresh changes of guests every six or seven days, Tom saw the visitors as the Pooles must have seen them, as on a moving scroll. Tom said to Jan, "This isn't a pleasant life."

She said, "It could be, but it's not for them."

One evening after dinner, while Tom and the Dodges played a game of darts in the lodge, an American threw a paperback against the wall, cursing. Pete looked at the book. "Stephen King, *Insomnia,* page five-fifty-four, eh?" Alan was nearby, doing his math homework.

"Yes," said the American. "How did you know?"

"It's a goddamn crime!" shouted Pete. "I can't stand this anymore!" He grabbed the book.

Tom saw Alan watching his father while pretending to keep his eye on his work.

"Here it is, you were on page five-fifty-four, and then the next five pages are missing."

"Right," said the American. "But how did you know? I brought this book with me. It's not your copy."

"They're all the goddamn same, mate. All the same. It's how they print them. And obviously no one complains, that's what scares me. No one complains! It's the world. It's the whole badly made world. That's why I came here, to get away from the badly made world, but it follows me. It follows me."

The American looked at his book. "It was printed this way? A few pages didn't just fall out?"

"That's what I thought the first time. That's right. I thought, It's the glue. But it's not the glue. I've taken these books apart, it ain't the glue. It's the printing. Alan, how many is that?"

Alan looked up. "I dunno. Fifty?"

"Try seventy-five."

The American didn't understand, exactly, and Pete explained. "They're printing them badly. Missing pages. Some books are worse than others. It's mostly the popular writers, your Stephen Kings, your Elmore Leonards, your Patricia Cornwells. They can't print 'em fast enough, and they get greedy and sloppy."

The American put a hand on Pete's arm. "It's just a book. I'll get another."

"Sorry for the temper," said Pete. "Let me buy you a drink."

On the sunset cruise the next day, Tom asked Alan what was really happening with the books.

"Why are you asking me?"

"I saw you looking at your father yesterday. While he was yelling, you were happy. I hadn't seen you smile until then."

"Why are you watching me?"

"Tell me about the books."

"They're badly printed."

"You've seen seventy-five books with missing pages? I haven't."

"You don't read the right books."

"I saw something in your eyes when your father was

talking. Contempt and satisfaction. That's a brutal combination in a sixteen-year-old boy."

"He told you his story, did he?"

"Yes."

"Leave Australia, follow your dream, make money doing what you'd do for fun? That story?"

"Yes."

"And you think it's a good story."

"It might be. I couldn't tell."

"I can't help you."

...

A few nights later, Tom sat on the *Mimesis* deck, looking at the stars, when he heard Alan on the beach, talking to a British nurse who had been on the *Mimesis* the day before. She was in her late thirties and, unusual for the Reef Club, alone. The men had circled her from the moment she arrived, because she was independent and easy to look at, but she kept them at a distance, eating with the group but returning early to her bungalow. And perhaps the men hated her for not letting one of them into her bed.

Their voices weren't clear, but the two of them, the boy and the woman, frightened Tom, and he was curious about what his fear would uncover. He slipped down the swim ladder and swam to the beach to get a better view. He hoped his movements would be lost in ripples. He crawled onto the sand and listened from behind a tree.

UNDER RADAR

"Oh, God, it must be neat to live out here," said the nurse. "Really neat. Swiss Family Robinson, my my my, how delicious, now pure. I'm probably the first person to say so."

"Not the first."

"I can't imagine how many times people have told you that you and your mom and dad are the Swiss Family Robinson, that you're the child boy Friday, or Peter Pan in never-never land, or Huckleberry Finn. I can't imagine. And until tonight, no one has ever said so to make fun of you, have they? What'll you write in your journal tonight? 'Dear Diary, she was making fun of me and she was mocking my mother and father.'"

Alan said, "Well, the island is all I've ever known."

"I know who you are. You don't have to be so polite."

Alan was quiet. Tom knew the use of silence as a weapon in these latitudes, letting the atmosphere fill in the spaces. Warm breezes muffle the need to say whatever is on your mind. Tom hoped the nurse wouldn't use the silence to excuse herself, to get back to the bar.

"How old are you?" she asked.

"I'm sixteen."

"You know who you remind me of?"

"No."

"Of course not. You don't know who I know. But I'll tell you. My husband."

"You're married?"

"We're getting a divorce. As if there's any other reason for me to be here alone. I could have a boyfriend if I

153

wanted. But not now. Maybe you, though? Huh? Are you my new boyfriend?"

She stood up from the bench and walked into the water, up to her knees. A coconut fell, pushing dry fronds aside and then landing with a thump. Overhead, fruit bats whistled.

"It's so disgustingly what it's supposed to be," she said, "but this isn't a pretty island. It's not like Bali."

"That's what people say." Alan joined her in the water.

"Oh, I insulted your pwetty pwetty island. I made a big insult. So sorry. Have you been to Bora-Bora?"

"No, but people say that's prettier, too."

"Now, that's a beautiful island. That's a classic. There's no grandeur here."

"These aren't volcanic islands. Bora-Bora was a volcano."

"Whatever."

"I'm sure a lot of places are prettier than Fiji. I've seen the pictures."

"And your mommy and daddy haven't taken you to any of them."

"Not yet."

"Ah, yet. Yes. So there's hope."

"Someday. When I'm older. My parents don't like to travel."

"You've never left the island."

"Yes. I've been to Suva. I've been to Viti Levu. I've been to the Yasawas."

"Those are all islands in Fiji. You've never been to New Zealand or Australia?"

"No."

Silence for a moment, and then she asked, "Do you know why I left my husband?"

"Maybe you'd better tell me."

"Because he's just like you."

Up at the lodge, a man began to shout, "No, no, no, no, no."

The woman asked, "Why are you smiling?"

"It's a nice night."

"It's always a nice night here. That's not why you're smiling."

"I don't think you're being very fair to me."

"Fair? Was my husband fair to me?"

"I don't know. I never met him."

"He loved me, but there was someone else. Of course there was, but otherwise he was perfect."

"I'm sorry."

"What were you doing with my book?"

"I was reading it."

"You're lying. I don't know what you're up to, but you're lying. My husband is like you. You have the same aura he did at your age, and I know because I met him when I was your age. We were together for a long time. I'm going to try not to let those years turn into a waste because of the way they died. It actually doesn't matter to me, really, whatever it is you're up to. Just remember this moment for the rest of your life, that someone busted you for who you are."

"Why are you saying all of this to me?"

"As if you didn't know," she said, and she slapped him across the face. The noise surprised both of them, and she said "Ah" as though she hadn't known her rage until she felt the sting on her palm. Tom could feel the pain in the noise, and then Alan cried.

"Shut up," said the nurse.

"It hurts."

"What do you know about pain?"

Alan ran up the steps to the lodge. The woman yelled after him, "Don't play your little game, you son of a bitch. I know what you're doing. I know who you are." She yelled that thought a few times, and then returned to the water, and sat down. The water came to her breasts. She muttered to herself, "I know who you are. You can't fool me."

Beryl Poole was running down the steps to the beach as Tom was about to leave his hiding place. Alan was with her. The nurse heard them but stayed where she was. Beryl walked through the water and faced her. Alan followed.

"Alan, tell me again, what happened?"

"She hit me," said the boy. He fell into his mother's arms for a hug.

"That's disgusting," said the nurse.

"What did you do to my son?" asked Beryl.

"It's between us."

"That's not an acceptable answer." She asked Alan, "What did you do to start this?"

"I didn't say anything. She's crazy. She says I remind her of her husband. And she slapped me."

His mother said none of this made sense. She looked down at the nurse. "Why did you slap him?"

"You can lie to me, you can lie to him, but you can't lie to yourself."

"I don't know what happened, but you're drunk. Go back to your room. You're not happy, and we want our guests to be happy. We'll put you on the morning plane and pay you back for the days remaining."

"Why was he in my room this morning?"

Beryl asked Alan, "Were you working?"

"Yes."

Beryl explained. "Is that what this is about? My son works. He's not like the boys where you come from. He works. He has a key and does a job here."

"Why was he tearing the pages from my book?"

Beryl had no answer.

Alan looked down the beach and saw Tom in the moonlit shadow behind the tree.

When Tom returned to the boat, he told Jan and Eddie what he had seen and heard. No one could make sense of it.

"He'll be here soon enough," said Tom.

In an hour or so, the boy paddled his blue kayak to the *Mimesis.* Eddie tied the line to a cleat, and the boy was with them.

"What was that about?" asked Tom.

"It's impossible to explain."

"If it really was impossible," said Eddie, "then you wouldn't be here. You want to tell us. So tell us."

"You don't know about my parents," said Alan. "What would you think of them if I told you they came here to kill the Fijians?"

Jan said she wouldn't know what to think. "I might think hard about why their son would tell such a story."

"It's the truth," said Alan.

Tom said, "I think I believe you. Why don't we just listen and decide for ourselves."

"Based on what?" asked Eddie.

"Based on what he tells us," said Tom. "If it fits what we already know or what we already suspect."

"All right," said Jan. "I won't interrupt."

Jan made tea, and the three gathered on the soft hammock between the boat's hulls.

Alan waited for them to settle and began his tale. "Killing the natives. That's what they expected to do. There was no date. Something had to happen in the world first, an apocalypse, the war of all against all. And this anticipation didn't begin with my father, it was a family tradition. My father's father was American, like you, and he came to Australia to escape everything that was evil at home. He wasn't looking for a farm and self-sufficiency, he just hated the Jews and the blacks. He was disappointed in Australia. It wasn't different enough. When he died, he said it hadn't been worth the change.

"My mother and father met in university. They fell in love because they were both politically right-wing.

There weren't many like them. They believed in the gold standard and in a flat tax. The flat tax was everything. They set up card tables outside campus events, asking people to sign petitions in support of the flat tax. Next to the signature you had to put your phone number, and later, one of my parents would ring you up and ask to see you. They wanted converts to join them in the Australian Flat Tax Association, AFTA. I think they finished with about twenty people in the group. They all wrote letters to the newspapers, offering the flat-tax solution to every social problem. The AFTA men wore a white shirt, a tie, and pressed pants. They were careful to turn at right angles when walking in public. Everyone knew they were crazy.

"My parents' inability to register enough new members to the group convinced them that the message of truth would never spread, because people don't want to save themselves, because people love being slaves to a progressive tax system that punishes the people who work the hardest. That a nation could live in slavery to such an unjust system was proof to my parents that the end of the world was coming, a political end, not a religious end. They finished university and had to make a living. They bought a map store from a woman whose husband had built the business but died suddenly, at fifty-one. My parents didn't know much about maps, but they saw possibilities in the business. The store did well, actually, better than they expected, because they hated it. They hated getting up in the morning and hated closing the shop at night. They hated all of the mail. They hated paying bills. They hated it so much that they worked harder to save the business from their contempt for it.

"But it was one step in the service of a goal. They wanted to live on an island and build a retreat for others who were like them. I don't know whose idea it was, but they settled on a resort for expert scuba divers, and they'd never gone diving themselves. A dive resort instead of a regular hotel because the guests would come bringing their own interests, and the resort wouldn't need to tell people how to have a good time. Very methodically, after my parents learned to scuba dive and became experts, they traveled around the South Pacific for three months, visiting every island that had a good reputation for diving and at least a grass landing strip for small airplanes. They settled here on Taveuni, to be near the coral fans. At the end of the second year, I was born. As my father likes to say, I'm the boy he wanted to be and he's the father he wanted to have.

"To an outsider, I'm sure my childhood looked perfect. I had freedom and responsibility. From the beginning, I had work to do at the club, and I could go alone anywhere on the island. All my friends were Fijians. There were a few white children, but I never felt part of their world, because my parents stayed out of their parents' society. The other innkeepers. That world. Rum at five. Lots of affairs. It wasn't what my parents were here for. They barely drink. When I was thirteen, my father told me, 'We're going to kill the Fijians someday. I don't know

when. And you're going to help, you'll have to. The collapse of civilization will make peace between the races
impossible. There's others we know who'll come to the
island and help us. Every race is going to fight every other
race until one race stands alone. I'm sad about this, I don't
hate anyone. I don't hate the Fijians, they're wonderful
people. If they weren't, I wouldn't let you play with them.
But they have to die, otherwise they'll kill you, and me,
and your mother. And you don't want that. One day the
whites on this island, even the people I don't talk to, are
going to wake up to their necessities, and we're going to
gather all of the darks and put them in one place on the
island and kill them. And you'll help.'

"I asked if my mother knew this. He said she did.
My mother, in her dedication to the organizing power
of the end of the world, had calculated the likely damage
the island would suffer after the seas rise when the icecaps
melt. On her reckoning, they built the resort up on the
bluff instead of along the beach. Not that she expected
tourism when the waters rose, but other white people who
washed up onshore would need a place if they were fit to
be kept alive.

"What my father forgot was that I was born here.
He shouldn't have told me his plan, because I was one of
them. I am a native Fijian. So it was my responsibility to
save my people from my father.

"One afternoon when I was fourteen, while my father was on the dive boat and my mother was at the airport meeting the plane, I went to one of the guest rooms

to steal something. I found a gold Rolex hidden inside a running shoe. I watched the bungalow when the diver came back from the reef that night. It took about fifteen minutes, and then he began screaming and ranting, and called for my father and accused the staff of theft. My father said the staff was honest, but the man persisted because the watch had been in the toe of the shoe, hidden behind the sock, and the sock was on the floor. My father asked him why he hadn't used the safe, and the man said that safes are broken into. My father said, 'And shoes are sometimes stolen,' and the man said, 'Yes, and so are watches.' So my father called for Ako, the housekeeper, who my father was desperate to believe was innocent, because if Ako was a thief, then the Fijians were just like everyone else, and their deaths would have no tragic glory, and when he killed them he wouldn't be playing out a tragedy, he'd just be slaughtering children. So I was happy, because his vision of the world was melting. And if it wasn't, at least he was miserable, and that was good enough for me. I was sorry for Ako, that was my only guilt, when my father went with the owner of the watch to Ako's village and complained about her to the Chief. My father told him that if word got back to the tourist world about the thieves of Fiji, business would disappear. 'And what then?' he asked. 'And what then?'

"The chief beat Ako, and she cried, and I wanted to throw up. I ran home to the club, took the watch from where I'd hidden it, went back into the man's bungalow, and tucked the watch into one of his other shoes. He apologized to my father in the morning and gave him a hundred dollars to give to Ako, but my father made him apologize to Ako directly, and to her chief. It was a mess, everyone on the island knew the story.

"My father wanted to kick the guest out of the hotel, but my mother said that this would only make for trouble, and the man was contrite.

"I waited two weeks for a new set of guests to be flushed into the hotel, and I stole a good dive watch. The owner complained, and my father told him he'd investigate. Two days later, the watch appeared under the man's pillow, and he told my father that he'd found it. My father said to me, 'That's the second time this month.'

"And then there was the third, and the fourth, and more. I stole watches, knives, and cameras. When the guests reported the thefts, my father told them to look again while he made his own investigation, which of course he didn't, and then, sure enough, everything always came back. My mother suspected the staff, but after watching them closely and asking me to watch them as well, we agreed that no one was stealing anything.

"'People weren't always this forgetful,' said my father one afternoon.

"My mother agreed. 'Whatever it is, I hope it's not catching.'

"To make it catch, I needed a simple delivery system for the virus. It was Stephen King who showed me the way. One day someone left a copy of *Insomnia* on a table in the lounge, with a postcard for a bookmark. I went back to my room for a double-edged razor I'd kept from one of my thefts, and I very neatly sliced five pages from the spine; the first of the cut pages was two pages from the guest's bookmark. The page on the left ended in a thought that seemed to continue on the right. I hovered around the lodge that night, helping my father at the bar, until *Insomnia*'s owner opened the book to the postcard. I watched him as he struggled with a sudden loss of meaning. He stopped, read ahead a few pages, read back. What had he missed? Why was the book losing any sense of itself? What was wrong with Stephen King? He read ahead again, to see if he could pick up King's hidden meaning. Then he saw the gap in the page numbers, and he started to swear. He threw the book away and went back to his room. My father asked, 'What was that about?'

"I said I didn't know.

"After this, I sabotaged every novel I could safely grab for a few minutes. I knew which pages to cut in the complete works of Tom Clancy, John Grisham, James Ellroy, Patricia Cornwell, Anne Rice, and Elmore Leonard. When the readers stumbled over the gaps, they went crazy. After the moaning and groaning, they threw the books against walls, into the trash, into the fire when we had one.

"My poor father; everyone was out of their minds as far as he was concerned. The world was sending him people who couldn't keep track of their brushes, combs, and watches, and the world couldn't print a book. It all made sense. There were gaps everywhere now.

"'The mind of the world is turning into Swiss cheese,' my mother said. 'The world is getting stupid-sloppy.'

"My father included this insight in his usual declamation to new guests. 'It's happening all the time. That's one of the reasons Beryl and I left Australia. We could see it all coming. And it's the little things, you know, spelling errors in advertising, or your book getting to the bookstore with pages missing, that are the real signs to me that the so-called civilized world that you live in is heading for a terrible fall. And they accept it, that's the horror, they accept that in their forties their minds are going senile, and they don't even have long enough memories to complain, they don't remember what they've lost, to try and make changes in the world." And there was a sentiment he stopped expressing. He used to say, 'I'm not saying that island life has all the answers, but it's a better place to be raising a child.'

"But he didn't believe this anymore. The decay of the world, in these tiny manifestations, convinced him that the spreading plague had poisoned everything, had poisoned Fiji. My parents hate the guests now, and the whole endeavor of the club is becoming a bore. They think better of the natives, who forget nothing and lose nothing, because they have nothing. So they deserve the island to themselves. Because of a few pages missing from a horror novel, my father is ready to abandon his dream of massacre. I showed him that the white world has nothing left worth saving.

"'The world is dying,' he told me. 'And I'm sick of the Reef Club. I don't know what to do.'

"And he probably wouldn't have known what to do if the nurse hadn't found me in her room this morning. When I saw her heading to the dive boat, I went to her room, but I didn't know that she had sprained her ankle stepping into the launch and decided not to go. She was coming back into her room just while I was slicing a few pages out of *The Vampire Lestat*. I couldn't cover for myself, the pages and the blade were in my hand.

"She asked me why I was in the room, why I was holding the book and the blade. I said I found the blade on the floor. I said I was changing the lights, that it was one of my jobs, going around the rooms to change the lights.

"She said the lights were fine.

"I said that one of the maids had said a light was out and I was checking on it.

"And why didn't I have a replacement bulb?

"I said I wanted to see which bulb was out.

"She said they all looked like the same kind of bulb to her. What about the book?

"I said I was just taking a peek.

"Anne Rice, she said, was too spicy for a boy my age.

"I said I knew that, and asked if she would leave the book with me if she finished it.

"She said no. 'What about the pages,' she asked.

"'Oh,' I said. I picked up the book, and the pages fell out. 'Books are very badly made these days. Ask my father.'

"'And he's an expert on printing?'

"'He has a theory about the world, and it starts with books.'

"She told me to leave her alone.

"I found an empty hut where someone was reading *Insomnia,* and sliced one page.

"That was this morning. You saw the rest. I feel badly for my mother. You saw me get her to hug me, Tom, when the nurse was yelling at me. My mother was ready to trust me, but when I hugged her, she recognized a strategy. She may have held me close, but she was someplace else, the same place she goes the hour before sunset, after the guests return from the water and before they hit the bar. In that hour, my mother can sit on the lodge's veranda and drink her tea and watch the cloud shadows on the lagoon. By the time the blue sky is flame, the guests are already drunk. Although my father needs to show his face before dinner, my mother has, for years, withdrawn from the guests' predictable excitement over the display. It was the sunset, the view, the daily worship of just that sunset and the satisfied melancholy it allowed which had drawn my parents from Australia, but selling it to the guests spoiled something.

"Degraded by the drunken ovations for the sunset, the sunset became a movie my parents had seen too many times. Leaving the sunset to the guests, my mother learned to settle her account with the day a few hours early; she became a connoisseur of the late long shadow. This was as close as she came to religion."

"That was some hug," said Jan.

Eddie asked, "Did your parents say anything about the books?"

"They didn't have to. I saved my people, you know, but at the cost of my family. This is good-bye." And with that, he climbed into his kayak and paddled home.

The *Mimesis* crew sat up talking about him. "I wouldn't have done the same," said Jan, "but what else could a boy do to protect himself against such a murderous father?"

"But his father didn't kill anyone," said Eddie. "It was just his fantasy."

"He told his son. And his son couldn't have known that the father was so weak."

Tom thought to say, But that's just what the son knew. He kept his tongue since it was only an interpretation, and no more right than any other. Wanting to know the rest of the story, he went to the lodge in the morning, in time to see the nurse leaving for the airport. Half an hour later the plane took off, passed over the lagoon, leaving the island quiet again. Alan and his parents sat on the veranda. A copy of *The Firm,* torn in half, lay on the floor.

The phone rang, and Beryl answered, then put Alan on. Tom walked away, already taking leave of the island. He knew their stay was over.

It took a week to stock the boat with food and gear for the trip to Hawaii, and in that time they saw Alan only from a distance. Jan tried to talk to Pete and Beryl, but they retreated behind the wall that years of professional courtesy had built. They could play the roles they'd made for themselves without ever letting whatever was real in them, if anything was still real in them, from showing through.

The last good-bye was formal and friendly. Tom asked the Pooles to remember him to Alan, but they didn't say they would.

Pete said it, "We're selling the club. We're going to travel."

"The three of you?" asked Eddie, looking for trouble.

"Alan's going to school in New Zealand to get ready for university."

"We'd like to say good-bye."

"We'll tell him."

...

The *Mimesis* had been at sea for two days when Alan climbed out of the spinnaker bag.

"I'm sorry," he said. "I couldn't go to New Zealand. I couldn't go to school."

"This is bad," said Eddie. "I have to take you back."

"Please don't," said Alan. "They want to get rid of me, and now I'm gone. They don't care."

"This is kidnapping," said Jan.

"But they don't know I'm here. Before I slipped onto the *Mimesis*, I took a skiff and towed the kayak into the channel and let it go. They'll have seen by now that the kayak is missing. They'll figure I paddled away and either killed myself or was washed overboard by a wave. They won't look for me with you. I have a lot of skills. I can fix anything. I want to see the world and pay my own way. I have my passport. I'm old enough."

Tom doubted this, but Jan and Eddie accepted what the boy said.

"Will you ever look them up and tell them what happened?" asked Jan.

"I haven't thought about it."

"Someday, when you're older and you've learned to forgive them, you should find them and tell them about yourself."

"I'm not ready for that yet."

Tom asked why he didn't want to go to school in New Zealand.

"They put me on the phone with the school's rector. I couldn't stand him. He asked me about the books I've been reading and how they had gotten to an island without a bookstore or library; what team sports I'd be interested in playing at the school; and whether I was really fluent in Fijian, and if I was, would I speak some to him, because he spoke Maori and he wanted to see if they were close. I told him about the nurse in Fijian, but he didn't understand. I can't go there. I can't go there. I know it. I just can't."

On the watch that night, with nothing between the boat and Hawaii, Tom thought about the headmaster and what he must have said, and what he might have thought of this boy. Tom imagined that the man would have worried about Alan's years on the island, between cultures, neither American nor Australian nor truly of the old colonial society, leaving him with a distant perspective and no solid self, no single identity inside of him, no source of confidence to build connections to new people. Tom imagined that an insightful headmaster would see Alan as an unfortunate loner, too old to be changed by one year of school. Tom imagined that the headmaster would try, though, because that was his job. Tom assigned the headmaster a wife whose grandfather had a mission in Tonga, where her father still ran an inn.

He imagined the headmaster saying to Alan, "My wife loves the islands."

To which Alan responds, "You don't?"

"Oh, when I was young, yes. I don't need to see them anymore. I've been there, you know? Palm trees, lagoons, the whole advertisement come to life. And the sun, I'm afraid I had a bit too much when I was the vagabond. The little moles on my back are spreading. If we knew then what we know now about melanoma, I would have worn long sleeves all the time. Anyway, that's all past. Now, when we can, we head straight to Sydney, and every other year we visit friends in San Francisco. New Zealand is backwater enough and island enough for me."

Six

The outboard grumbled in the swell as Tom climbed into the dinghy. The waves, five feet, small whitecaps, pitched the rubber boat into the *Mimesis* and lifted the screw out of the water. Spinning in the air, it made a desperate complaint. Alan, sitting low in the stern, held fast to the tiller. Tom rode in the front for balance.

"Are you sure you can make it back?" asked Tom.

"I grew up on the sea. This is nothing."

Jan gave Alan the handheld GPS with the catamaran's position already set. They would meet back at this spot after Alan dropped Tom at a safe place in Honolulu Harbor. Then the *Mimesis* would enter the harbor, where Alan and the Dodges would register with customs. If Tom's passport, when it went through the American computers at customs, betrayed him as a felon convicted overseas, they would all be in trouble.

Tom knew there might even be a warrant out for his arrest, but not for the murder. Someone from the old Paul Farrar days might have come clean about the crime, or one of the good marriages unraveled and, in the rending, a lawsuit over community property unburied a numbered account, and too much money, and taxes due. Tom, a convicted murderer, could have taken blame for the whole conspiracy. Better to drive him up into a harbor in a small rubber boat, under radar's sweep of the sea. Even if the *Mimesis* was spotted by the coast guard, the inflatable was invisible.

With a signal from Jan, Eddie kicked the *Mimesis*'s diesel into gear, and the cat made headway, against the chance that a twist of the sea would bring the dinghy hard against one of the hulls. They were safely away, and under power, the boat accepted the weight of the men gracefully and rode the waves with less anxiety.

The men had nothing to say to each other. They took comfort in the silent agreement to be silent. Both of them were wet. Tom sat on a garbage bag stuffed with dry clothes and his shoes. He never wore shoes on the *Mimesis,* and they were going to feel strange on his feet.

Alan held a pair of binoculars. Three container ships, a half mile apart, waited to enter the harbor. Tom studied the ships and then pointed Alan to where he guessed the last ship would be in fifteen minutes.

Now everything went the way they had hoped.

The big container ship, their guardian, never knew the service it performed. Blazing lights on deck, the massive thing slowed down as it entered the channel. The little rubber boat, with no lights running, followed beside it past the breakwater. Alan steered the dinghy under the ship's lifeboats, hiding them from anyone on deck. By instinct, the two men crouched low and whispered. Alan studied the harbor with his binoculars.

"We have a problem," he said. "There's a fence around the port. We have to find a place where you can be let off and not cause attention. And there's a coast guard station here, which means security. Better get dressed."

Tom stripped and dried himself with a towel from the garbage bag. Then he put on long pants, a tropical-print shirt, socks, and a pair of running shoes. The dinghy bobbed in response to his movements. They were close to the big cargo cranes, but they needed a small-boat marina, yachts, sailboats, a dockside restaurant.

"Let's just cruise," said Tom. "Anyone can cruise."

They left the cargo ship. The piers were tall, and there weren't many ladders to the water.

What would they look like to anyone watching? Two boat bums on a ride from one piece of business to another. The dinghy moved with the forward energy that gives a passerby a little pulse of envy to see someone pushing steadily ahead on the water. Tom remembered the first time he'd seen the dinghy as he helped load the sail bag.

"This is the best we can hope for," said Tom, pointing to a floating dock beside a salvage yard, and a rotting cabin cruiser, *Carpe Diem,* settled uneasily in the water, her paint blistered and flaking, her brightwork rotten. "There are no businesses over here. And look, there's a bike path around the yard, and the boats are locked behind a fence. This is the place." He wanted to let Alan go back to the *Mimesis*. Jan and Eddie wouldn't rest until Alan was with them, and he had a lot of sea to cover without the ballast of another man to hold the dinghy steady.

"How do you feel?" asked Alan.

"About?"

"Coming home."

"Is this home?"

"It's America."

"I don't have to close the circle?"

"I don't think so."

Tom stepped to the dock. Alan reached up with his hand. "I'll see you."

"Tell them I'm fine," said Tom.

Tom walked quickly up the gangway as Alan returned to the open sea.

Aside from any other considerations, thought Tom, the chance for arrest, my strange destiny, Alan's prospect for disaster in the waters between here and a catamaran five miles from the shore, this is fun.

He slept that night in a twenty-dollar room at a seaman's hotel near the water. He walked to Waikiki in the morning, the ground rolling under his feet. He was land-sick now, after so many weeks at sea. It was going to last a few days, and a walk would help him recover. And he was happy to walk. He was happy about everything.

In the afternoon, he met Jan and Eddie and Alan at the bar of the pink Sheraton on Waikiki. They had passed customs easily but endorsed Tom's caution.

What a quartet! They looked famous, and all those who were watching studied them, trying to make sense of their aura of fame. What was the white-haired man to Jan and Eddie, and they to Alan? The four emanated confidence, a friendship stronger for survival of an ordeal, but what tribulation? They must be musicians, was the secret assay, and then those who stared, out of respect, stopped looking.

Meanwhile, the four of them were just having a good time, rollicking sailors grateful for shore and another round of drinks. Jan watched Alan finish his third rum. "I didn't know you had that facility."

"I'm learning."

"I don't know. Maybe you're falling apart. That takes talent. Here you tell us the story of your life and you sound like a man with insight for a dozen, and now look at you. A sunburned rummy in a fancy bar."

"You rang?" said Eddie.

Tom wasn't drinking.

"I'm going to stay and be a beachcomber," said Alan.

"Every tropical resort has a hotel called the Beachcomber," said Eddie. "Think about it. Or a bar. Or two. The Beachcomber. The Vagabond. What do I say? Right. I'm drunk. Oh yes, this. Does anyone know what a real beachcomber looks like? He's an unsteady drunk! He's a man who gives so much thought to such local issues as the destruction and interment of memory that he becomes a university of one. Like you, my dear," and he set his watery eye on his wife.

"Are we fighting?" she asked.

"Getting drunk and letting off steam. We've been cooped up. Everyone's got a right. Tom, you got a right. Let it go. Get drunk, too."

"No," said Tom. "I don't want to."

"Eddie," said Jan, "d'you want me to leave you? D'you want me 'a stay in Hawaii and let you finish the world by yourself?"

"No, why?"

"Because I'm not convinced of my own integrity anymore."

"Oh."

Alan giggled.

"What's 'at for?" asked Eddie. "Huh? You want to stay here? This is not a cheap place to be. You can't just drop anchor here and pay the natives a couple of dollars for a bushel of passion fruit. This place costs money. Ain't no barter in Hawaii. This isn't Rancho del Nada on the Costa del Nowhere."

"I can manage," said Jan. "Tom'll sail to Mexico with me tomorrow."

"I don't know about that," said Tom.

"You don't want to go with us?" They had been teasing each other, but Tom was serious, and Jan stopped playing.

Eddie signaled to the waiter for another round by stirring the air with a finger pointed at the table. "Tom, you're not going to stay here. We're in America now. We'll hit the California coast, anywhere you want, and you're free. We can leave in a week. It'll take us three more to get there."

"I don't think so," said Tom.

"Why?" asked Eddie.

From the bar he could see the hotel's gift shop, where two teenage girls tried on sunglasses from a wire rack. They were sisters; Tom guessed the younger was starting high school, and the older would be just finishing, or a freshman in college. The little one bothered the big one to approve her shades, and the big one was too busy for her, but she turned to indulgently dismiss the younger by saying yes to the sunglasses before giving them a serious look. The younger, busy like a parakeet with her reflection in the rack's small mirror, wanted only that yes and didn't whine for real attention or sincerity.

Their mother came out of the dressing room of the shop, wearing a tropical-print dress of big orange flowers and green stalks on a white field, and the girls returned the glasses to the rack, running to judge the dress and each granting to the mother the enthusiasm they had just denied themselves. It was a silly resort dress the woman would never wear at home, too busy and unrefined, but in its very wrongness for home, the dress made the vacation that much more of a costume parade, and who doesn't love a parade? Their mother asked the girls a question, and they pulled her to the sunglasses rack, and she bought them what they wanted. Spending money easily, they shared a vacation's license for pleasure.

Tom knew them. The mother was Rosalie, and the girls were his daughters. Tom made a quick calculation. Perri was nineteen, and Alma was fourteen.

The drinks came.

Tom excused himself. He went to the bathroom and looked in the mirror. His nose was broken. His hair was white. He had a beard. The face in his passport, ten years younger, how close was it? Who was that lawyer in a tie? The man in the mirror was gorgeous, in his face a shifting balance of agony and generosity, the tensions of a saint, but the man in the passport looked like a hundred thousand others. A woman could live with Passport Tom for the quality of a man's reliable devotions; she would make peace with that face of dull symmetry, though her reach for higher love and closer friendship be thwarted. But Passport Tom was a secret criminal. He wondered, had Rosalie loved him for his secret life without knowing why? What part of her suspected his sins yet honored his self-control, that he could steal and still help the girls with their homework? Had she married him for the reasons that Paul Farrar chose him as an accomplice in the fraud, for his vicious greed under such bland skin? Married him with her own hidden double ceremony, a marriage between her private life and his? So had he betrayed her secret alliance with his secret soul by inventing an insult and then losing control over nothing? But it wasn't nothing, not then. His daughter had been raped, in a way.

But only in a way. The man in the mirror would not

kill for the same reasons. But he might kill for others. Tom wondered, Would I still be a saint?

In the mirror, he saw wisdom. In the passport, he saw no tact, no indication of manners refined enough to be religious. In the early face, there was no misery. There was still the face you see when you lean your head against the window in a train and you look through it to a river, and then you come into a tunnel, and for a moment you see yourself reflected in the window with the darkness behind, and you see how dull you are, how dulled by the world, how transparent, how focused only on yourself, how you consolidate the world only in your reflection, the constant repetition of all your narrow thoughts drawing a silhouette, the shape of your head the outline of the world's missing purity. Now, in the hotel bathroom mirror, the difference was this: the face he saw in the mirror would know the tunnel was coming, it was just that kind of face, sagacity obvious and clear as a Gershwin tune, that face he saw would never be caught staring blankly out at nothing, into nothing. In his new face, he beheld no capacity for boredom, so his wife would never recognize him.

Certainly the girls would never know the face of the man in the mirror. He would walk past Perri and Alma, to smell the air they filled, to inhale them. Had their mother allowed the girls a few photographs of him beside their beds? Daddy with the baby in his lap, Daddy swimming with the baby. Daddy with the girls on a ski slope. Daddy at the soccer game. Daddy and Mommy in Halloween costumes.

What did they remember of that day in the Jamaican waterfall? Perri at nineteen, a freshman in college, what college? And Alma, fourteen, what is that?

"I can see them," he said. "I can take the risk."

Tom walked to the lobby.

Rosalie and the girls were getting into a taxi. There was a man with them. Tom saw only his Hawaiian print shirt and khaki shorts. The taxi driver closed the trunk, filled with suitcases.

Tom went to the head of the taxi line and told the first driver to follow Rosalie's cab. "I think they're going to the airport."

"International or interisland?"

"I don't know." Tom had ten dollars in his wallet.

Rosalie's cab took the exit for the interisland terminal. "They're going to another island," said the driver.

"It's my wife," said Tom. "She's with another man."

"And you just found out?"

"I've been following them."

"You're not going to get violent on them, are you? I don't want that in my life. I don't want to drive you someplace and then you hurt someone. I'm a gentle person."

"I won't."

"But you might. I'm going to let you off now so you can't find out where they're going. If she wants you to know, she can tell you."

Tom agreed with the driver, who pulled to the side. "No charge."

"I appreciate that."

"You don't know a thing, you don't know she's with him, you don't know who she is. Don't make this the disaster of your life."

Tom thanked the driver, and then he ran to the terminal. He was desperate but not crazy. He knew what he was, and it made sense to him. There was something he had to do, find his family. But why? What did he want from them? What would he do? That he couldn't just introduce himself to Rosalie, that he couldn't just sweep his daughters into his arms and absorb them into his love and regret; that he knew better, had this restraint, he now suffered to understand, was part of the problem. He could not easily insert himself into the drama of his family's life on a vacation, or, God forbid, a honeymoon!, without ruining his daughters, and yet there was a man with them. Who was he? His wife had remarried. Sure. Of course she had to find another man, to give his daughters a father, and the man would be a good man, she would have made certain of that. His sister would have made certain.

But even his sister could be fooled again.

Rosalie came from a family of professionals, with doctors and lawyers in the family tree like apples at harvest. It took Tom no longer than two seconds at the hotel's entrance to mark that the gestures of the man who got into the taxi with Rosalie and his daughters were ir- refutably correct. Even the hair on his tanned arm was decorous. She had found a mandarin.

But I am not sucking on my artificial sobriety any- more, thought Tom. I can drink if I want to.

He wondered why this sentiment intruded.

Because, because you have very little time to make yourself known to them, because you are wise now and can trust that your impressions of someone go directly to the heart.

With each step, as he ran faster, he felt cooler, and when he reached the terminal, he registered no change between the humid windy air outside the building and the dry chill within. He trotted past the ticket counters, stood in the line for the security check, and was through.

His daughters were together at a frozen yogurt stand.

Easy to walk up to the counter. His daughters smelled of shampoo and something else, not perfume, he was sure, perhaps a scented water, something they'd sprayed on their faces from a sample bottle at the hotel gift shop. Or was it just their sunscreen? It didn't matter at all, but he wanted to know, just to own something precise about his children.

They were talking about music, about a band, the name meant nothing to him, and he was happy for them in the way they shared enthusiasm. They were beautiful, he was sure of it. Their tanned skin alarmed him, but if the vacation was over, why weren't they on a flight to the mainland? So they're tan. No, he thought, they're on a tour of the islands. They've been here a week. He had a chance, but he didn't know for what. The woman behind the counter asked him what flavor he wanted.

He looked to the girls. "What's a good flavor?"

"Chocolate, I guess," said Perri.

"Or mango," said Alma.

"Then I'll have a double scoop, one of each." Neither girl turned to his voice as though hearing the resonance of an old bedtime story.

The girls didn't care and passed away from his warm, indulgent smile, although Perri studied him for a second because he looked so interesting, so severe, perhaps.

He followed them, which was easy to do in the crowd, and when they joined Rosalie and the new man at a gate for a plane to Maui, he left the terminal and went back to tell the news to his shipmates at the Sheraton bar.

"And you want to go to Maui," said Eddie.

"Yes, I'll go to Maui and I'll find them."

"Don't be so sure," said Eddie. "There's a lot of hotels on that island. And don't forget the condominiums and houses for rent. It may not be so easy to find them. Maybe they're staying with friends. You'll never find them that way."

"They're at a hotel," said Tom. "I saw the man's watch. It was expensive and not a common brand. He's used to indulging himself. They'll stay at a hotel and, I'd wager, the most expensive."

"A bet?" said Eddie. "You don't have the money."
He winked, which meant, We'll take you there, and
let's get on the boat now, because we don't have much
time.

...

"What will you do once you find them?"
"I don't know."
"Will you announce yourself?"
"I don't know."
"You have very little money."
"Seven and a half dollars. I had ten, but I bought a
frozen yogurt. "
"Seven and a half dollars isn't enough."
"I'll manage."
"You need a haircut and a shave. After you pay for
that, you'll have nothing left. Let us pay for that."
"Thank you. I will."

...

The wind blew twenty-five knots on a purple sea of swells
running eight feet high. He asked for the wheel and, guid-
ing the boat on a broad reach, with the wind coming from
the side, put the boat over the waves. Ahead of him was
Maui, the final landfall with his old friends. He pointed
the boat towards Lahaina, sitting above Maui's waist, where

the island narrows to a plain between two dead volcanoes hidden in cloud. A fringe of hotels stretched along the coast.

While Tom looked at the place that might, at last, reveal his destiny, a whale broached the surface and slapped the water with its tail. Jan, Eddie, and Alan analyzed the vision; was it an omen? Did they believe in omens?

"Seeing the girls was the good omen, it forecast that we'd see the whale," Tom said. If luck or chance brought the girls to him once, why not again?

Jan took his binoculars. "Look what they're selling. Printed T-shirts and beach hats to honeymooners and second honeymooners."

The cheap ugliness of the place, too easy to ridicule, netted surfeits of contempt from the other three that strained Tom's affection for them. I don't want to hear this now, he thought, my children are out there somewhere, and a cultural critique gets in my way. This is how people live today. What would you rather see, slaves in the hot sun? I will not despise or condemn. Let me get rid of my protective shell, let me remove whatever remains of my defenses, let me suffer the various buffetings and impressions that come to me, let me be aware of life without judgment today. He was annoyed with his friends and cold about it. Well, he thought, so there is no constant, single achieved feeling of balance and goodness, only a faster ability to correct one's course and shield one's heart against mindless damage. I am the ship, and I am also the reef.

They lowered the sails, and Eddie brought the *Mimesis* to a mooring.

This was going to be their final good-bye.

"Well, well, well," said Eddie. He put a hundred-dollar bill in Tom's hand. "You've been a wonderful addition to my life, Tom. Whatever your past, whatever your future, remember that on this little boat, in fair weather and foul, you had real friends, people who knew you and liked you and loved you. Go with peace, and may whatever challenges you meet along the way turn into blessings."

It was Jan's turn. "I never told you all the many stories that I should have, and now it's too late." She held him, crying.

"No, no," said Tom. "Don't do this to yourself."

"I can't help it. Regrets, regrets, regrets."

"Why?"

"Because there might be something that I know, something I could have shared with you, that could save you in the future. It's like the fairy tales where someone is given three special gifts that make no sense at the time, a gold ball, a feather, a piece of glass, and then each of those gifts becomes that thing that saves the hero's life at three times in his life and makes his quest a success. And I have so many stories, and one of them might have had the power to rescue my poor Tom, and I call you my poor Tom because of what I can see of your heart. Broken, broken, broken."

"But I like it this way," said Tom. "Don't cry for me.

And I'll always remember you, and who knows, maybe one of the stories you already told me gave me the weapons I'll need when everything else has failed."

"Do you think so?" asked Jan.

"I hope so," said Tom.

And now Alan offered Tom his hand, and when Tom reached for it, Alan clasped Tom around the neck and hugged him. Tom saw a bad end for Alan, a lonely death, drowned, probably, thrown overboard, but not by the Dodges, by someone else. Alan's gloom would never lift, for all the reasons he had become this wreck so young in life.

So they let Tom off at the end of a fuel dock, to continue on their way around the world.

Tom waved at them as the dinghy returned to the *Mimesis*. "I will never see you again!" he called out, the words bouncing off the sound of the outboard.

With nothing in his hand but a hundred-dollar bill, he walked into the next part of his life.

...

The best remedy for distress is work, sudden wealth, or a beautiful woman. I have none of this, thought Tom, but I will create relief by a kind of parallel agreement. My work: to find my children. My sudden wealth: that I know where to look. My beautiful woman: but here Tom ran against the fence of his reality. He stroked his chin, felt his beard, found a barber, and changed himself once again.

He bought a Maui guidebook, then fruit, cheese, and bread, and ate under an old tree in a park on the Lahaina waterfront. The most expensive hotels on the island were the Ritz-Carlton, the Four Seasons, the Grand Wailea, and The Palace of the King.

What was her name? Was she Rosalie Levy or did she use her maiden name, was she Rosalie Desser? If she was married to the man in the taxi, she would have taken his name, but would the girls have changed their name? Would she have asked them to sever that connection to their father?

He called the hotels and asked for Perri Levy.

She was staying at The Palace of the King.

"May I ask who is calling?" The hotel operator knew the name too quickly for someone who had just checked in the day before.

"I can't hear you," said Tom.

"May I ask who is calling?"

Tom hung up. Why was Perri screening calls? Why did the operator take no time to look up his daughter's room number? If Perri was a guest, why did the operator guard her with the familiar nerve of a longtime servant?

What defeat awaits me? he wondered.

Do I have a right to seek them out?

Yes. God put us here. What else is one of the names of God but the secret opportunity behind coincidence?

It was two o'clock. The afternoon wind lifted the tops of the palms and the flags along the waterfront, and

there were so many of them, ornamental and national.
Away from the *Mimesis,* and his need to take an argument's
other side for the sport of conversation, Tom watched the
tourists with diminishing compassion, and when he felt his
contempt rise, he challenged himself to find a better spirit.
However this would end, he would refuse the tragic. His
daughters were somewhere in this mob of the mottled,
the obese, the oversugared, the desperate for diversion,
the alcoholic, the numb. Do not hate anyone, he told
himself, at least not yet. Just feel the grief for the lost les-
sons you could have taught your daughter if only, in
Jamaica, ten years ago, your attribute of mercy had sup-
pressed my attribute of rage. The tourists know so little,
he thought, and then he beat to another tack, but the
thoughts were equally close-hauled, because the tourists
were also, if not pure and innocent, certainly less guilty
than he of murder, most of them, and he suspected—but
then changed suspicion to wonder, did the murderers
among them keep the same distance from the cheap parade for the same reasons as he? All of this bad taste, this
smothering of something that might be real or better,
contaminated the world. But now he could ask if he belonged to a negative aristocracy. He summoned his
foul mood from the Montego House, and the recovered
memory of his disdain for the style of the place cut him
with a long, cold blade. As deep as he thought he had gone
in his repentance, there was a further revelation and yet
another punishment: had mediocre design, bad decora-
tion, and people with no sense of fashion driven him to

murder? What a waste. It was a thought to pursue, but he had his daughters to consider, so he accepted the world as it was given to him.

He walked the six miles from Lahaina to the hotel, not to save money but to let the rhythm and purpose of his stride help find a channel for his calculations. If his daughters were happy, and if his restoration would hurt them, be the death of their futures by the return of a buried past, the embalmed come back to life, he would withdraw.

So he marched on, left and right, left and right, planning with one set of strides how to approach his daughters as though his life would continue with them; and then with the next set of steps, he calmly imagined scenarios of happiness without his daughters, the ways to live out the rest of his time as a life and not a judgment. He would have a specific life if he failed to be his daughters' father again, he would make specific friends, learn a technical skill.

But I don't want to be without them, he thought. That was the truth.

He took the beach path for hotels east of The Palace of the King, along a trail that linked the big resorts and separated them from the sea. The ocean, whitecaps flocking across the channel, offered danger to even the best swimmers. Under a broad, windy sky, the sheltered hotel pools were crowded and easy to invade.

The Palace of the King was the prettiest of all, the hanging gardens of Babylon, three towers joined by bridges, set above a terraced jungle. The center tower's roof supported a green world all its own. To the left, facing the hotel, the lowest of the pools was built in the style of a lagoon, with a sandy beach and, in the middle, a sunken galleon that held a bar. A long water slide delivered shrieking children from the next terrace. To the right, a wide lawn surrounded a pagoda. And there was a Japanese couple getting married! On the terraces above were more swimming pools, lined by Greek columns. Or maybe Roman. What difference? It was classical, and quiet. Everywhere flowers bloomed, and the air was rich with the scent of gardenia.

He walked through the lobby, all white marble, an atrium open to the sky fifteen floors above. Sheer pastel curtains broke up the space; through one scrim was the reception desk, through another a bar, and there, a gift shop. The effect was instantly calming and exciting, it was playful. It made Tom happy to know his daughters were here.

He returned by another set of meandering steps to the lagoon pool, where Perri and Alma, on submerged stools at the galleon bar, sipped from straws in pineapples, wearing the sunglasses they'd bought on Waikiki. The sunglasses paid for by Rosalie. They looked perfectly content, twisting on their seats, at once pretending to be movie stars and surpassing the intimidating power of movie stars.

Rosalie's new man appeared behind the bar and kissed each of Tom's daughters lightly on the lips. Since the shipwreck bar was in the middle of the pool, Rosalie's new man must have entered through a hidden passage. The bartenders joked with him with a deferential familiarity, which he reflected back as appreciation, and by the way he restrained himself from an equivalent joviality, and by the command he took when he entered from the submarine passage, Tom understood that Rosalie's new man was either the owner of the hotel or the senior manager. And he was there just to talk to Tom's children, this was not an inspection tour.

Rosalie's new man refilled both of their drinks himself. They adored him.

My wife has married a king. My daughters have become princesses.

Is the marriage new?

They could be living here now.

If they're living here, I have time.

If this is a short visit, if he owns many hotels and they're here for a quick vacation, then they'll leave and I won't be able to follow them home so quickly, although I can find out where they live.

If I had died and, after ten years in limbo, awoke bodiless at this hotel, spirit witness to my children's new life, wouldn't I look upon their new father and fortune as a gift?

Let me see if this is good or bad.

Tom slept that night at a Little League field, in the dugout along the third-base line. He still had fifty dollars.

He walked back to the hotel and sat at the foot of a banyan tree on the other side of the path from the hotel, where he could see the lagoon pool.

He prayed for guidance. He needed a simple vision, a small plan, a tiny idea, nothing larger than a postage stamp, really, from which to begin his trip back to his daughters. This is a meditation. I will relax my eyes and make no distinction between the metal bands around the palm trees, the light on the eyelashes of the waitress bringing that plate of onion rings to those nanny-attended children, the Hawaiian tenor with the high sweet voice on the bar's sound system, and the woman using her room key as a bookmark before she takes to the water.

Tom walked past the woman's shoes and stopped to tie his laces. He grabbed her key and moved back to the banyan tree, where he waited.

The woman returned from the pool, and Tom followed her back to her room. He rode with her in the elevator to the ninth floor of the west tower. When she turned right, he followed and then walked ahead of her, listening to her steps. She came to her room, W914. She opened the book for the key and swore.

She knocked on the door, and there was no answer.

She returned to the lobby.

Tom used the key to open her door and went into the room.

There was a camera on the desk, loaded with film. He put the camera on a shelf and set the timer, then took a picture of himself. He finished the roll by taking pictures of the room, the clothes, the safe, the shoes, and then, when the film rewound, put the film in his pocket and left the room.

He had been in the room for three minutes.

His daughters were at the pool again. He hadn't yet seen Rosalie.

Three men sat together under the awnings of a cabana. Tom sat nearby, listening for a name. One said to another, "Bill, you don't know. You just don't know."

When Bill left, Tom followed him to his room in the central tower, C1200, a suite overlooking the water. Tom went down to the health club, called the hotel operator on a house phone, and said, "Hi, this is Todd at the spa. I have an appointment here for Bill something-or-other in C1200, but he's late. Could you spell me the last name?"

Bill Delantash.

Tom then went to one of the cafés near the pool and sat at the counter. The waiter recognized Tom because he had been hovering in the area for two days. Tom ordered a sandwich and signed for it using the name. He filled in the room number, C1200.

He slept again in the dugout at the Little League field.

In the clothing store, he charged two shirts to Bill Delantash, and a bathing suit, and a hotel robe. With the hotel robe, it was now safe for him to sit on a chaise by the pool. The men were still there, still in the cabana.

Rosalie and the girls passed him on their way into the ocean. He took his time and went to the beach, where Rosalie and the girls stood in the water up to their waists. The girls faced the ocean, and Rosalie completed the triangle, facing the hotel. Her eyes skimmed over Tom. He felt her disregard for him, another single man at the beach watching her sexy daughters, his gaze an attack on their beauty. He wanted to say hello, to unmask himself right there, tell her the truth about himself, about his travels. He wanted to forgive Rosalie her rage at him, absolve her of the time she wasted hating him, he wanted to let her know that absolution would mean permission to know that her pain needed no excuse, only that the pain had long passed its profit. She would have the right to bring him forward into the world and make him confess his sins again, without the guarantee of her reprieve. She could say No. What then? If he begged her once in public to forgive him, and she said No, and then he gathered another audience, distinguished citizens all, their friends and family, and begged her again for mercy, and she said No, and then he found another court of opinion and recited all of his sins, all of his offenses, all of the ways that he knew his actions had defamed his family, ruined his daughters, shattered the vessels of the world in which they lived, and Rosalie, upon hearing his humble agonized plea for release from his punishment, yet one more time coldly said No, well then, would the sin be upon her shoulders? And so he forgave her that sin now and wished the reciprocal turn from her.

Which did no good, of course, since the dialogue was all in his head, while Rosalie looked through him to the hotel, in expectation, Tom guessed, for her husband (yes, her husband, there was the gold band on her fourth finger), due any minute now for their late-afternoon swim in the ocean.

Tom withdrew from the beach. The curse of his journey, his powerful face, forced him to hide. If he stayed for too long, his singular beauty would stay with Rosalie, and were she to see him again, suspicion of the truth, that he was following her, would cause her alarm.

From the promontory in front of the next hotel, obscured by bushes, Tom watched Rosalie's husband run into the ocean and grab her. They kissed. His daughters splashed water on the two of them, and then Rosalie's husband returned the splashes. The new husband and the daughters then swam together away from the beach. The reef, a long way off the shore, kept the waves from breaking closely, and the three swam safely, lazily, joking.

There was nothing to interpret.

Tom returned to the dugout to sleep. He sat up for the night, marveling at life's parade of dilemmas, this infinite battalion of choice and consequence.

If I . . . then she . . . then they . . .

If I . . . then he . . . then she . . . then they . . .

The next morning, Tom was in the lobby early. Already a fixture in the hotel, he was careful not to stay for long in any one zone, and to make few demands on services, eating lightly. Rosalie's new husband crossed the lobby and chatted with the people working at the front desk. When he passed, Tom asked a bellman, "Is that the manager?"

"He's Mr. Cohen, the owner."

"John Cohen?"

"David."

"Ah," said Tom.

Tom called to make an appointment to see him in two days. He explained to Mr. David Cohen's secretary that he was calling from Los Angeles, that he was with a film production company and wanted to talk about using the hotel as a location for a movie. The secretary asked if he would speak instead to one of Mr. Cohen's managers, but Tom allowed that he would need only a few minutes of Mr. Cohen's time, after which he would approach the manager, but since Mr. Cohen would have to approve this anyway, could he at least explore with Mr. Cohen the possibility of using the hotel as a location. "I only need five minutes."

She put him on the schedule.

For the next two days, Tom avoided the hotel and Lahaina, anyplace where Mr. David Cohen might see him. He left the film of the room he had invaded to be developed by the hotel's photo store.

On the day of the meeting, he showered at a public beach, dressed in the bathroom, and walked to the hotel. Along the way he bought a portfolio case at a stationery store for twelve dollars. He put the photographs inside, along with the receipts for everything he'd charged at the hotel.

The hotel's administration offices were on the second floor of the west tower. Tom introduced himself as Lyle Monaster. He was kept waiting for half an hour, which he expected, and then admitted to David Cohen's office.

Cohen greeted him with the affable expectation of a busy man. The office was quiet. The room had the restrained pastels of the lobby. There were photographs on the wall, an exhibition of Cohen's life, with a suite of pictures taken with Rosalie and the girls, starting, Tom estimated, two years after he went to prison.

"David Cohen."

"Lyle Monaster," said Tom.

"Can I get you anything?"

"No, thank you."

"You're from Hollywood."

"No."

"I was told you want to use the Palace as a location for a movie."

"Let me show you something." Tom laid out everything from his new portfolio, the photographs of the hotel room and all of the receipts.

Cohen looked first at the receipts and then the photographs. He reacted calmly. Of course Tom's manner and face belonged to a man deserving respect, but still, he had just dealt a puzzle.

"Lyle," said Cohen, "I think you're trying to help me."

"I'm trying to show you something."

"You're from the security company."

"No. I work alone," said Tom.

"Tell me what all of this means."

Tom thought of Jan Dodge's last words to him, about the fairy tales and the precious objects that have meaning only as each solves a problem in the story.

"These are pictures of a room I broke into using a stolen key. These are receipts for meals and clothes that I charged to someone's room. I haven't stayed here. I just walked in from the beach."

"Why did you do this?"

"It's my business."

"You're not telling me everything."

"No."

Cohen called his secretary. "What do I have next?"

She listed his appointments.

"Call them and reschedule. Tell them I'm sorry. Don't explain." When he finished with his secretary, he asked Tom, "Now what?"

"Your security is excellent. The amount of money you'd have to spend to prevent this kind of theft is more than you would lose without my help."

"But what about the cost to public relations?"

"Well, that's always the problem, isn't it?"

"And you're still not telling me who you really are."

"Why do you suspect me?"

"I don't," said Cohen. "Actually, I feel very close to you."

"I'm glad for that."

"I don't believe what you're telling me about yourself, but I trust you. Why?"

"I don't know."

"But you know what I'm talking about, don't you, Lyle?"

"I think so."

"What is it about you? People tell you everything, don't they?"

"Some do."

"More than some."

"You've committed a crime, haven't you?"

"I don't know how to answer that question."

"Yes, you do. Tell me the truth."

"I'm here to prevent crime."

"Crime that's too small for me to bother pursuing but enough to hire you to stop it, yes? You didn't learn about this kind of crime in a book, did you?"

"I studied."

"You studied on the job. And you've been in jail."

"How does it show?"

"You're as clean as a nun. That's how I know. Men out of prison are often beautifully clean."

"Were you in jail?"

"Close enough. I'll ask you again. Have you ever committed a crime?"

Tom said nothing, not to hide the truth but to give Cohen a taste of unsettling silence.

"Never mind," said Cohen, "I see that you want me to go first. Fine, then. Here's my story. I used to be a doctor. Not many people know this. This was fifteen years ago. I had finished my residency, in orthopedics. Someone approached me and asked if I wanted to make a lot of money quickly. I asked him how he dared to approach me this way, and he said that I was the type who said yes. He described the situation to me, and it made sense. So I said yes, because I knew that just to be chosen by this man meant that I was already guilty.

"He set me up as one piece of a large insurance fraud. None of us—and we were doctors and lawyers—knew the full extent of the crime, we all knew a few others in the conspiracy, but only the leader, the man who selected us, had the whole picture."

"And your wife, did she know?" Tom nodded to the wall of pictures.

"I wasn't married then."

"Does she know now?"

"Yes, she knows everything. I told her everything."

"Were you arrested?"

"God, no."

"You said you'd come close to jail."

"If I'd been arrested, I would have been convicted. That's close. But I wasn't arrested. I prospered. I made millions. Not then, but from the investments. The man who organized this made it a condition of the conspiracy that we stop after we had reached a certain amount of money. When that milestone passed, the thing ended. None of us could carry on alone, because none of us knew how all of it worked. My job was to provide reports of broken bones. Someone else filed claims with insurance companies. I never even knew which insurance companies were paying. I think he was working with someone inside a company. Any of us might have attempted a crime like this, but none of us had the nerve to do more than our small part. Now you know."

"What is it about the photographs I took and the meals I stole that made you want to tell me your story?"

"I don't know. I just did. I felt that if I hadn't, you'd have found out anyway."

"So you carry the guilt."

"For a long time, my bad feelings about what I'd done overwhelmed me. Not the terrible paranoia of being arrested. The statute of limitations has passed, and the organizer died."

"He died?"

"He had a bad heart. He came to see me, I referred him to a specialist."

"So now you're free."

"Not really. I'm not a doctor anymore. I couldn't practice medicine after the scam wrapped up. I tried, but having used my art for crime, I couldn't retrieve it for its original purpose. I couldn't trust myself with my patients, with the choices I had to make, to help them. I didn't believe my diagnoses. I was acting the part of the doctor. I was trained in surgery, but I couldn't make the incision."

"How long after this stopped did you quit?"

"It was a few years. By then, some investments I made started to grow. The market was good in those days. I looked for a business, one thing led to another, and I bought a few hotels. Now I have ten. This is the flagship. We lived around the country for a while, but now we're here, my family and I. I give a lot to charity," said Cohen. "This doesn't atone for my crimes, not completely, but it helps."

"The woman you married already had two children."

"Yes. How did you know?"

"I see their pictures on the wall. You ended the crime before you were married, but the girls are as old as the crime. The older one, certainly."

"Yes. Rosalie, my wife, was a widow. It's a terrible story. Her husband died in Jamaica."

"An accident?"

"Something like that."

Tom said nothing.

"No, not something like that. I'm being evasive. He murdered a man while they were on vacation. No one has ever been sure of what happened or why. He went to jail and died there."

"How?"

"He was killed in a fight. After he died, the man who brought me into crime introduced me to his widow. He said I could be good for her."

Now Tom wasn't sure if he was alive anymore. Had the prison reported his death after the fight in which he broke his nose? But this didn't make sense. Or maybe when everyone was released from the prison, there had been a fire and a riot, and all that he recalled of those days was a memory from death. Maybe he really was dead.

No. I'm alive, and I'm sitting here. When we were released from prison, was the word sent back that I was dead, to avoid a problem with the family or any kind of diplomatic trouble? Or had Rosalie told David Cohen that her husband was dead?

That was it. The world shifted to allow room for this piece.

Why did Rosalie love criminals? Because Tom and David were both men with an unplaceable sense of balance and power, moral strength, though it came from the immoral? Because an unredeemed piece of creation waited for Rosalie's help, and with Tom's refusal to accept his wife's love, the grid of destiny brought her to a man with courage equal to his guilt? From a lawyer to a doctor, from the betrayer of justice to the betrayer of healing?

All of this was braided and invisible.

"Hire me," said Tom.

"What will your job be?"

"I'll protect you. I'll continue to protect you. I'll monitor your security."

"Come to dinner. I'd like you to meet my family. Would you do that?"

"Yes."

Seven

Climaxes happen because something becomes intricate. Why, and when, do you make a mistake when you play the piano? What makes something difficult is not just the problem of dexterity. Have you ever noticed that even the simplest pieces give you difficulty towards the end? The music stretches out, and we anticipate the climax. The pleasure of the end scares us. We strain for release and block out the moment's sensations. We meet that place or point where the piece expands, where the music fulfills itself only by the way we tolerate the surge of feeling called for by a condensed run of notes, and we contract. But it isn't the difficulty that stumps us, we fail the challenge of emotion. If you don't realize that, you'll get used to the wrong notes.

Tom rode a private elevator to the roof of the hotel, where David Cohen lived in a secret glass house. Even the guests on the penthouse floor below were ignorant of the universal above them.

David Cohen looked upon Tom with an ancient affection, with fellowship, with pleasure. "You're going to be very good for me."

"I hope so. I hope this will be good for both of us."

"Of course it will. Here, let me introduce you."

Cohen brought Tom into the living room, from which the hotel grounds were hidden behind a hedge growing in large planters. The hedge admitted a view only of the ocean. Behind them, there was mountain. Rosalie and the girls were there, standing, waiting.

"Rosalie, I'd like you to meet my friend, Lyle Monaster."

Rosalie extended a hand. Where she had once been sucked dry by her first husband's ruminations and the weight of the two children, in the ten years since a stupid murder in a waterfall, love had resolved her distress. She was radiant now, calm and gracious. No one would want to harm her.

"Hello, Lyle."

"My pleasure," said Tom. He turned to the girls, such poised young beauties.

"This is Perri, and her sister, Alma."

"It's a pleasure to meet you," said Perri.

They shook hands. Her fingers were long, her nails were shaped and polished red, her hair was thick, she wore Tom's dead mother's pearls. Perri's hand was warm, and yes, still slightly damp.

"And this is Alma."

"And what a pleasure to meet you, Alma," said her father, for the first time in ten years.

"Welcome to our house," she said, also offering her hand. The touch was unfamiliar, but the hand was strong.

"You have a very strong hand," he said.

"I'm a gymnast."

"How wonderful."

Cohen, satisfied with his friend's manners, offered a drink.

"I'll have a glass of wine, please. Red wine."

This was his first drink since before he'd been to Jamaica, but it was time now, it was right.

Cohen nodded to his bartender, who poured drinks for everyone.

"Lyle is going to be working with me," said Cohen. "He's a specialist in security, but I suspect we'll find more for him to do than checking that the locks are working."

"Where are you from, Lyle?" asked Rosalie.

"My father was in the foreign service. We moved around the world. I'm American, but I've never really lived there until now. Mostly I've traveled."

"How exciting."

"What was your favorite place?" asked Perri.

"Jamaica."

A silence opened.

David Cohen met Tom's eyes with a question, but also with trust.

"We've been there. It's not our favorite place," said Rosalie.

"I'm sorry. People have different experiences wherever they go."

Alma asked him, "Why did you like it?"

"I heard a story there. Wherever I go, I hear stories, but this one was so mysterious that I could never quite forget it or ever quite understand it. Let me ask you, why don't you like Jamaica?"

"My first husband died there."

"This was very clumsy of me."

"You didn't know."

"I did, though. David mentioned it earlier, but your daughter asked me, and I wasn't thinking clearly enough to give a different answer."

"You told the truth."

"I could have just as easily said Paris or the Red Sea at dawn and spared you the pain. I'm sorry."

"What was the story?" asked Rosalie.

"Should I tell it?" Tom asked.

"My husband died a long time ago," Rosalie said. "David has been the father to my daughters. What happened then, when my husband, well, you must know."

"David said he killed someone."

"Yes. We don't know why. So perhaps a story about Jamaica is what we need to hear now, if you'll tell it."

Cohen supported Rosalie's bid. "My family is strong. Don't be afraid."

"I'm hungry," said Tom. "Perhaps we should eat first, and then you can tell me about yourselves, and after dinner, I'll tell the story."

As they walked to the dining table set outside in the garden, Tom stopped at a wall with pictures of the girls.

There was Alma, the gymnast, on a balance beam, on the uneven parallel bars, on a vault. And there was the picture of Tom and his girls, the last picture of them together in happiness, taken by Rosalie in Jamaica, Tom between his daughters, leaning over to fit the frame. Tom pretended to study the picture of Alma on the vault.

"How old were you when you started?" he asked her.

"When I was seven. That's late, but I caught up."

"You're good." He turned from the wall.

"I try."

Tom remembered the way she had taken such pleasure in dancing with the singer at the Montego House. And here she was standing on her hands, her legs spread wide. There was a compulsion in her that he never could have stopped. What had Barry Seckler done but recognize in the little girl her dream of performance?

They sat at a round table, with Tom between Rosalie and Perri. He was given the honored position, facing the ocean.

Perri had finished high school but had not yet applied to a university. She was working for David Cohen in the office, learning the hotel business.

"But you'll finish college?" asked Tom.

"Yes, I expect to. But I don't know when or where."

This is the effect of my disappearance. She depends on the stepfather because she misses me. She's afraid to leave home.

"And Rosalie. Do you work?"

"I work with a few charities. I volunteer."

Why did no one recognize him? Because I am not so angry anymore. Because I am not the center of the world anymore.

"We're stuck with life, aren't we?" asked David Cohen.

"That means I should tell my story," said Tom.

"Yes," said Rosalie.

Tom inhaled the air of this family. He thought of the witch who predicted his punishment. If he found her, he would thank her. Perhaps I should look for her. And then he opened his mouth, and listened to a story the hanged man told him, that he only just now remembered.

"In former days, when the children of Solomon were threatened by an evil decree, the Ras Tafaris would take the staff of Judah into the desert, to a special place, and there they would recite a certain prayer and make an offering to the Holy One, Blessed Be He. And the disaster would be averted. And when the staff of Judah disappeared, the Ras Tafaris would go to that place in the desert, and even without the staff, they still knew that certain prayer. And they would say the prayer, and the disaster would be averted. And when the special place was lost but the prayer was still known, they would recite the prayer and beg for help from the Holy One, Blessed Be He, and the disaster would be averted. Now the staff of Judah is gone. The path to the special place has been covered by sand. The prayer has been forgotten. But we still have the story. Tell the story."

After Tom finished the brief tale, his listeners held the silence.

Rosalie spoke first. "Thank you," she said. "I don't expect that any of us fully understand your story, but I don't think we have to right away."

"No," said Tom. "It takes time."

...

Perri and Alma, wounded early in their lives, wanted only happiness for their mother, who worked so hard to make them strong. They were too young to make sense of everything this white-haired man with the broken nose had to tell them, but when they harkened to his advice and followed his suggestions, life was easier for them. Rosalie went to him often, and the girls would see them walk together on the beach, talking, always talking. Their step-father accepted the stranger completely. In time they loved him, too, their mother's curious friend.

They listened to him tell her one night that the purpose of the gift of life is the discovery of our purpose. It would take a long time, or a short time, for that purpose to be known.

"One could fulfill one's purpose," they heard him say, "and live a long time after."

Their mother asked, "And then?"

He answered quickly. "And then you tell the story."